Empire
of
Serpants

Dragons of Isentol Book 3

RICHARD FIERCE

and

pdmac

Cover design by germancreative.

Cover art by Rosauro Ugang

ISBN: 978-1-947329-47-8

THANK YOU

To our wives, with all our hearts

Contents

CHAPTER 1

Gwen

The city of Haddence was a flurry of activity.

Gwen watched merchants pitch their wares, from brightly colored silks to food that permeated the air with their scents. Small children ran along the streets, playing a game and shouting at each other lightheartedly. It was almost enough to make her think that the impending darkness of Torian's madness was just a dream.

Almost.

Venia had landed outside the city and Gwen had walked from there. Despite traveling by air, which had been a living nightmare for Gwen, it had still taken two days to reach the city. Venia had a voracious appetite and continuously stopped to eat. She promised to be at the rebellion meeting, but Gwen wasn't sure how that would happen. Venia was massive, so unless the rebellion was meeting outside in a large open field, it didn't seem possible. The more pressing issue was that Gwen didn't know where the meeting location was, and it wasn't like she could ask someone, could she?

"Good day, madam! Wear the finest clothing this side of the border," a merchant said to her, producing an armful of elegantly sewn dresses. "I sew them myself." The merchant offered a grin that stretched his pockmarked face and revealed a mouthful of yellowed teeth. He was bald and slightly overweight, but his clothing was of high quality.

Gwen smiled and politely shook her head. "No, thank you. You haven't seen a group of people that seem out of place, have you?"

"I'm afraid not," the merchant replied, offering a wink. He tapped his waist where a bag hung from his belt. It clinked with coins.

The man's intent was obvious and Gwen retrieved a coin from her purse and offered it to the merchant. He swept his hand over hers and the coin vanished, but Gwen hadn't felt his touch at all. Was he truly a merchant, or some sort of vagrant pickpocket?

"Go to the end of this street and you'll see the butcher shop on the right. Beside it, there's an alley that'll take you to a door. Knock twice."

"Thank you," Gwen said. She continued along the cobblestone street, but she could feel eyes watching her. A glance over her shoulder revealed the bald man was gone, replaced by an elderly woman. Gwen thought it was odd, but she followed the man's directions anyway.

At the end of the street was the butcher's building, and Gwen found the alley. She stepped into the darkened space and walked twenty feet to reach the door. Gwen raised her hand to knock and heard shuffling behind her.

"Don't move," someone said gruffly.

Gwen froze. Her heart skipped a beat.

"Who are you and what do you want?"

"I'm here to see my friends," Gwen replied vaguely.

"Names, girl."

Gwen considered lying but decided not to. If this person was connected to the rebellion and she used a fake name, it could keep her from getting into the meeting.

"His name is Eradore."

"Never heard of him," the gruff man replied.

"Perhaps I'm in the wrong place. I'm sorry, I'll just be on my way."

"You aren't going anywhere."

Something sharp jabbed into Gwen's lower back and she sucked in a breath.

"Please—"

"Shut your mouth," the man said. He applied pressure on the blade and Gwen flinched. "Who sent you here? Torian? Grimmar? I'll gut you like a fish, you blasted spy."

Gwen barely heard his words. She was focused on the pulse of magic flowing through the fire rune. Her right hand grew warm as the flames started to form. The door in front of her opened and a robed figure stepped into view.

"What's this?"

"A spy. I was just about to show her what we do to spies."

"Gwen?"

At the sound of her name, Gwen cut off the magic and looked up to see Eradore. The elf was a welcome sight and she rushed forward and wrapped him in a tight hug. Eradore's surprise quickly faded and he patted her on the back, then pushed her at arm's length.

"Is everything all right? What are you doing here?" He looked down the alley, then back at her. "Where's Aimil?"

"It's a long story," Gwen said. "Aimil's a traitor."

"Come in," Eradore bade. "Tell me everything. As for you," Eradore turned his eyes on the guard. "You almost got burned to a crisp and didn't even know it. Next time, check for runes."

"Yes, sir," came the gruff reply.

Gwen turned to look at the man and saw it was the merchant who'd given her directions. He tucked his dagger away and offered a bow to her. "My apologies. Just doing my duty."

"Don't worry about it," Gwen replied. She stepped inside the building, and Eradore closed and latched the door.

"Speak as we walk. The leaders of the rebellion are about to convene."

Gwen related the events at Auleavell and Steepcross, leaving out nothing. She even showed Eradore her eyes and the dark rune lines that started at her collar bone. His expression was unreadable, but Gwen had the feeling that he wasn't happy about the dark magic. The two reached a small room guarded by a handful of warriors and a mage. When she finished talking, Eradore was silent for a long while.

"Where's the vial?" he finally asked.

"Marjorie destroyed it. She said it was too dangerous to give it back to me."

Eradore frowned. "If what you say is true, Aimil poses a great threat. She's been privy to many things within the rebellion."

"She also knows about me," Gwen said.

"What do you mean?"

"She was in the room when Marjorie told me my true name. Aimil knows I'm Kamron's daughter. I doubt she'll keep that information to herself."

"I think you're right. She's probably already reported to Torian. I wouldn't be surprised if Grimmar himself comes looking for you. Come with me. The others need to know."

The guards stepped aside to let allow them through. There were many people Gwen didn't recognize. A few familiar faces stood out and she was relieved when she spotted Lyra. Roland was also present. He'd been there when Tobias had fallen during the fight at the outpost. Seeing him brought back a rush of memories. Aimil had been there, too. The feeling of betrayal stung Gwen's heart again and she forced herself to swallow her anger. Aimil would pay. Dearly.

"We've come together to devise our plans against Torian," Eradore said, raising his voice to be heard over the scattered conversations. The noise died down and Eradore motioned to Gwen. "These plans will be greatly affected by the news that we have a queen to lead us. This is Quinlee, the daughter of King Kamron."

All eyes went to Gwen. She wasn't used to being the center of attention and she could feel her face flushing.

"Hold on!" It was a dwarf. Gwen looked at him, glad for the distraction. It diverted everyone's attention from her. The dwarf had thick curly brown hair and a long beard. He folded his arms across his chest and glared at Eradore.

"We don't need a queen to lead us when we've got a king." He thumbed toward a man behind him. Gwen was drawn to the man for reasons she couldn't understand. He was handsome and fit, with thick auburn hair and intense brown eyes.

"Who are you?" Eradore asked.

"Name's Torgreth. And his name is Conal. He's the son of King Kamron, and the heir to the throne."

"What proof do you have?" Eradore asked. "We have proof from the Great Library that this is Quinlee."

"And we have proof of the naming runes," Drustan spoke up, "that this is Darrbie, Kamron's only son."

The others in the room began trying to talk over one another until it was a mass shouting match. Gwen rubbed her temples. All the noise was going to give her a headache.

"Stop!" she shouted. "Everyone just stop!"

The room went silent and Gwen sighed in relief. "I don't want to lead us to war against Torian. I'm not a warrior and I know nothing of battle. I will defer to Conal. And if Conal is Kamron's son, that means he's my brother. There is no need for division among family."

Gwen looked at Conal and waited to see what he would say. She hoped he would agree to take the lead.

If she were forced into it, she was afraid many people would die due to the mistakes she would make.

Conal gazed at his sister. She was very pretty. Part of him wondered had they met in different circumstances as strangers whether anything would have happened between them. He shuddered at the thought and refocused. Yet here she was, both a stranger and a sister. He thought he should feel something, some sort of elation at the reuniting with family. But his family had been murdered and what he felt now had nothing to do with family.

"I accept battle leadership," Conal calmly said. Though his words were full of confidence, his expression hinted that he had some doubts.

"Thank you… brother." Gwen felt weird saying that. She'd been an only child her entire life. Yet now her long lost brother was here, in the same room with her. It was difficult for her to fathom. "What's the plan?"

Eradore looked at Conal. "Torian has many Prestiges at his command, but the Great Library's emissary has informed us that they will join our forces. With their Prestiges on our side, we just might stand a chance against Torian."

"We also have a dragon on our side," Gwen said.

"A dragon?" Eradore asked. "You didn't mention a dragon."

"Sorry. I wasn't sure how I should bring it up, but the dragon that brought me here promised her aid. Her name is Venia."

"We also have a dragon," Conal said. "We had two, but one was killed by dragon hunters."

"Do these dragons know each other?" Eradore asked.

"I'll have to ask her," Gwen replied. "She said she would be here for the meeting, but obviously she isn't here."

"Don't be so sure," Lyra spoke up. "Dragons can do many things, and that includes shapeshifting."

Gwen looked at Lyra curiously.

"It's true," Conal agreed. "I've seen it myself."

"Are you… Venia?" Gwen was being surprised at every turn.

"I am," Lyra, really Venia, answered. "Though you should use my elven name. My dragon name is personal and only given to those I trust."

Gwen remembered asking the dragon for her name in Auleavell and Venia had given it to her. She was humbled by the trust that such a mighty creature had in her and felt indebted somehow.

"With dragons on our side, we should easily be able to take Isentol back," Eradore said.

"Don't place too much hope in dragons," Conal counseled. "Yes, they are powerful, but very few remain... less than a dozen. And Torian has dragon hunters tracking them down. We've killed those hunters we found, but there's no telling how many more are on the prowl."

"Then it's probably a good idea to keep them split up in case these hunters make it into our camp somehow. Do you have a plan?"

Conal slowly nodded. "We need to keep Torian off balance. It seems to me that Gwen has the weight of magic on her side. I know nothing about magic. Therefore, I propose that we divide our efforts. Gwen and her forces attack from the east with all the magic you can employ. Force Torian to concentrate his efforts and attention to the east. My forces will wait until Torian is occupied with battling in the east… then we will attack from the west."

"I'll take Gwen to Auleavell to meet up with Kirith and his forces," Lyra said. "They're ready to march with us, he just needs to receive word before we arrive."

"That's easily done through magical means," Eradore said. "I'll have a message sent to Kirith."

"That begs the question of how do we coordinate our efforts once we are in position?" Conal asked. "We can't afford to wait for a messenger to get to us days after the fact."

"I have an answer for that, as well," Eradore smiled. "We have two mages that are connected magically by runes, but their bond is deeper than that. They're twins. Their sibling connection seems to have strengthened the power of the runes and they can communicate with one another over longer distances than usual. One of them will travel with Gwen and the other will travel with you."

Conal smiled. "Amazing things, these runes. That will work."

"What about the cities and towns along the way?" Gwen asked. "The people there are innocent and shouldn't suffer because we're marching through."

"I've thought about that," Conal said. "Anyone willing to join us is more than welcome. We can use all the extra bodies we can get. Everyone else can stay put and stay safe and out of the way. Most importantly, we buy everything we need along the way: food, supplies, even the ale. We are reclaiming a kingdom not punishing it. We want this to be as painless as possible."

Gwen was beginning to like Conal even more. He seemed to be a man of good intentions and she believed he would be a great leader in the aftermath of Torian's defeat.

"We can work out the minor details along the way," Conal added. "I think we should get moving. The quicker we are in position, the less time Torian has to prepare."

Gwen could feel excitement stirring within her. She wasn't a warrior but was ready to do what her people needed of her.

CHAPTER 2

Conal

Ignoring the usual after-meeting conversations, Conal focused on Gwen. Crossing over to stand before her, the difference in height became glaring. He towered over her by at least two hand spans, causing him to wonder how one set of parents could produce two children of such different sizes. Yet she was very pretty, her green eyes inquisitive as she returned his stare.

"So you're my sister."

"It would seem so."

"Where've you been?"

"I grew up in Dawsbury, right under Torian's nose. It's on the edge of Isentol."

"What did you do?"

"My father owned an inn." She caught herself, remembering the man she had called her father. A lump formed in her throat, but she didn't cry. The tears didn't come as often as they did before. "I served tables for him."

"An inn?" Conal chuckled, slowly nodding. "An interesting place to raise a king's daughter."

Gwen smiled in return. "What about you? Where did you grow up?"

"Urve, a coastal town in Tir Manach. My father was a jewelry merchant."

"Was?"

Conal's casual demeanor vanished. "He's dead. My entire family is dead. Torian had them killed."

"Torian's men killed my father. And my friend. His name was Tobias," she replied.

Eradore walked up, a man and a woman tagging along. "I know you two have a lot to talk about, but unfortunately, we're running out of time. These are the mage twins I mentioned, Kalan and Korla."

Conal suppressed a grin for the 'twins' couldn't be more different. Kalan was a hand span taller with dirty blond hair and brown eyes. He wasn't handsome as far as eye-catching, but he wasn't unattractive either. Yet there was something about him that immediately put Conal off. The man exuded a not so subtle arrogance.

His 'twin' on the other hand was a very attractive buxom strawberry-blond with an hour-glass figure, a little taller than Gwen. In contrast to Kalan's smugness, Korla looked like she felt out of place, her emerald green eyes darting around the room, taking everything in.

Conal silently prayed that Korla was his 'twin.'

"One of them will –" Eradore began before Kalan cut him off.

"I'll go with her." He thrust a finger at Gwen then nudged Korla towards Conal. "You can have my sister."

"That's fine," Conal replied a little too quickly, hoping Gwen and Eradore thought he was covering Kalan's crass behavior.

"You'd better get moving then," Eradore said, giving the oblivious Kalan a look of irritation.

Conal turned to Gwen. "See you in Havengarde. Take care of yourself."

"You too." Her eyes locked onto his and she smiled at him.

For an awkward moment, Conal felt he should do something demonstrable, like a hug or something, to show he recognized he had family again. But it would be like hugging a distant cousin he had met once growing up. He was about to give her the noncommittal hand wave when she closed the gap between them and hesitantly hugged him.

"Watch yourself," she cautioned. "Our uncle knows we're alive."

She didn't need to say anything else, for Conal understood. "Let me know where you're in position."

"I will," she answered, releasing him. She felt like there was more to say, but whatever it was, the words eluded her. "See you soon."

"You too," Conal replied, ready to move on. All the questions he wanted to ask would have to wait. He turned to Korla. "You ready."

"Yes," she shyly replied.

He searched the room and found Torgreth and Galadyr in conversation with Voldar and Lorkan, the elf with a bemused smile as he listened to Voldar relate some tale. Conal caught Torgreth's attention and soon the group was out in the streets and headed to the city gates.

"Where's Drustan?" Conal asked, suddenly remembering the half-druid-dragon.

"Last I saw him," Galadyr answered, "he was talking to Lyra."

Lyra… Conal remembered Drustan's words, *Two of our females have reached that age. It won't be long for the other four.* He wondered if Lyra was one of the female dragons who could still bear young.

"Speaking of which," Torgreth said, casting a sly look at Conal. "What's this 'we had two dragons, but one was killed' stuff? I've been with you for who knows how long and I've never even seen one dragon, let alone two… if they even exist."

"They exist, my friend," Galadyr replied.

Torgreth frowned at the elf. "You've seen one?"

"Yes."

"A dragon?" Voldar interrupted, cocking an eyebrow in disbelief. "You've actually seen a dragon? Simply saying 'I'm a dragon' doesn't mean you are one."

"If he says he has, then he has," Torgreth retorted.

"OK,OK," Voldar shot back. "What's with you?"

"He's an elf and elves don't lie. And even if they did, I still trust him."

"Thank you, Torgreth," Galadyr said, dipping his in appreciation. "I pray that I always have your trust."

"Yeah, yeah," Voldar responded, with a little twinge of jealousy. "What about the dragons?"

"How about we have this conversation in private, once we're outside the city," Conal interjected.

"He's right," Korla said, her voice soft and delicate. "There are too many prying ears here."

Conal noted that she walked behind them, doing her best to keep up. Slowing the pace, he motioned her to walk beside him.

"So, you and your brother can communicate even though separated by great distances." It was a statement rather than a question.

"Yes." She gazed up at him, smiling pleasantly. "It's a trait we discovered when we were very young."

Conal returned the gaze and smile as they walked. "And you're really twins?"

She giggled with girlish charm. "Yes."

"Who's the oldest?"

"I am."

"Were your parents surprised that they were having twins."

"No. A mage midwife had predicted my mother would have twins a year before she was pregnant."

"She predict anything else?" Conal pondered how he could spend more time with her without it looking too obvious.

"Just that we would be mages."

"You'll forgive me if I say that I have a hard time picturing your brother as a mage." This caused her to giggle again and Conal was smitten.

"He never did want to be a mage. Wanted to be a warrior, a soldier. Pa wouldn't hear it, especially after the midwife said he was going to be a mage."

Conal thought about it a moment. "Is he a mage because that is what he's really supposed to be or because your father made him become one and therefore the midwife's prediction is true regardless of his desires."

Korla stared at him as though he had plumped the depths of a divine mystery. "You are the first person ever to understand that. I've thought that all along, but never wanted to say anything because it would just make father angry. Besides, now it's too late for him to be anything other than a mage."

"I understand."

"I think we're far enough away from the city now," Voldar said with a knowing grin at Conal who glanced around, realizing they had passed through the main gates and he hadn't even noticed. "You can tell us about dragons now."

"Hold that thought," Lorkan announced, seeing a runner headed his way, a young man moving at a good clip.

"Commander," the young man greeted him, catching his breath. "Sorcha's intercepted a large force and is falling back towards us. She asks for immediate help."

"I thought she was at least two days north of us," Conal said. "We'll never reach her in time."

"We need to try, m'Lord. She's a resourceful commander, but she can't hold out against Torian and what remains of Caldyr's army."

Conal's lips pursed. "This is not how we intended to begin. We need Torian's attention in the east." Narrowing his attention on the messenger, he asked, "How did you get this information."

"Message hawk."

"M'Lord," Lorkan corrected.

The young man's eyes popped wide. "M'Lord."

"How long did it take for a hawk to get here?"

"A couple of hours… m'Lord."

"A couple of hours?" He was about to say that was impossible when he recalculated that a hawk could average 30 miles an hour. That would put Sorcha around 60 miles away. With a forced march, they could be there in two days.

"Your orders, m'Lord?" Lorkan said.

Conal thought quickly. "This could still work. If Gwen can move her forces by the time we connect with Sorcha, it might still work." Turning his head to look at Voldar, he said, "Why wasn't the dwarf commander with us in the meeting?"

"He's a prickly one. Gets his felling hurt at the drop of a hat. Near as I can see, he was waiting for a royal invitation from you."

"We don't have time for games," Conal growled. "Lorkan, get ready to move. We go to help Sorcha. You two," he said to the two dwarves, "let's go have a heart-to-heart with Storri." Not forgetting Galadyr, he said, "Would you mind finding out where our druid is?"

"As you wish," Galadyr replied with a respectful nod.

"What about me?" Korla piped up.

"You go with – no, change that. You come with me." Conal increased his pace, the dwarves and Korla quick marching to keep up.

As they made their way to the dwarven camp, Voldar leaned in to Korla. "The commander's name is Storri Broken-nose. You'll understand when you see him. One thing you gotta watch out though is not to slip up and call him 'Snorri.' As you can imagine, he doesn't like being reminded of his nose."

"It can't be that bad," she replied.

It *was* that bad when they stepped into Storri's tent and he looked up from behind the small field table he as using as a desk. Storri's nose looked like it had been hit with a smithy's hammer across the bridge for it was nearly flat, the nostrils like two eruptions on both sides.

"We missed you at the meeting, Commander," Conal said, doing his best to stare into the dwarf's eyes.

"I wasn't invited," he harrumphed.

"You don't need an invitation," Conal emphatically said. "You are an army commander. How am I supposed to plan and organize when the battle captain of half my force thinks he needs to be invited? When I asked King Rorkyn for support, he promised me he would send his best soldiers with his best commander. So you see, I need input from Rorkyn Orefell's *best* commander."

Assuaged, Storri cleared his throat. "Yes, well… all a misunderstanding, I'm sure."

"Good. We need to move out immediately. Sorcha is under attack and needs our support. If you will ride with me, I'd like to go over what we discussed in the meeting and get you input."

Flattered, Storri stood up and barked out orders to get ready to move then cast a look of authority at Torgreth and Voldar. "What are you two lollygagging around here for? Go find your regiment."

The two exchanged a worried glance as neither knew to which regiment they belonged. Besides, they had no clue what it meant to be a dwarf soldier. They liked where they were, hanging out with Conal.

"With your permission, General," Conal intervened. "I'd like to keep these two with me as liaison officers representing you. They know the operation and would be beneficial to me as the campaign proceeds, acting as messengers between you and me."

Storri harrumphed again and furrowed a thick brow at them. "Alright, m'Lord. If you can put up with those two, that works for me. Saves me the trouble of finding suitable liaison folks."

"Thank you. Well then, I'll leave you to get your army ready. I'll send one of the liaison officers to find you to let you know where I am."

Once outside, Torgreth sidled up to Conal sighing a big, "Thank you."

"That was very diplomatically played, m'Lord," Korla commented, impressed.

"We don't need personalities interfering with our battle plans. I meant what I said in there. I need him."

As Conal led the way to where Lorkan's army was lining up, he turned his head to look at Korla. "Can you contact your brother and tell him what's happening?"

"What specifically, m'Lord?"

"That we've been forced into attacking earlier than we had planned. She needs to get her forces in place and engaged as quickly as possible." He turned his head to see where he was going. "And my name is Conal."

"I know, m'Lord," she replied, her voice almost a coo, "and I am flattered with your familiarity, but you are still a king's son, a prince, and I am just a mage."

Conal slid his eyes to the right to catch a glimpse of the beautiful woman striding next to him. *You are far more than just a mage. Are you playing hard to get? Is there a man in your life?* He was about to ask when she bent her head, staring at the ground as they walked.

She abruptly stopped, causing the others to stop.

She frowned in puzzlement and tilted her head to look up at Conal. "I don't understand. He's not responding. The only reason for that is that his mind is focused, concentrating on something else so much that he's not listening."

Conal's jaw tightened and he resumed walking, shaking his head. *What's the point of you being here other than as a distraction if you can't communicate with that idiot brother of yours?* "This is *not* good. If it doesn't work now, what makes you think it will when I really need it."

"I'm… I'm sorry, m'Lord," Korla fretted, taking three steps to his two to keep up.

"Forget it," Conal replied though his irritation was evident. "You can try again later."

"Yes, m'Lord," she replied, lowering her eyes.

Conal was about to fuss at her to stop calling him 'm'Lord' when a runner from Lorkan raced up.

"M'Lord. Commander Lorkan says Sorcha's forces are a day out. She is surrendering ground faster than she can retreat. Commander Lorkan says that it is imperative that you give the order to march."

"Tell him to do so," Conal replied, breaking into a run. "Tell him we force march until we get there."

CHAPTER 3

Gwen

"I've never seen a dragon before," Kalan said eagerly.

"If we don't defeat Torian, you won't see one again," Venia said. Her words sounded like a reprimand, but Kalan didn't seem bothered.

"Do we need to get supplies before we leave?" Gwen asked. "Food and water?"

"No need until we reach Auleavell," Venia answered. "We'll make several stops along the way, and I'll make sure it's near civilized places so you two can get what you need. I'll fly high enough that no one on the ground should see us, but that requires a lot of energy and strength, which in turn requires a lot of food."

They walked along the main street, headed toward the gates where Gwen had entered. The rebellion spy was at his vendor stall, calling out to passerby and holding his dresses out for visibility. Gwen locked eyes with him as they passed and he offered a nod. When he'd cornered her and pressed a dagger to her back, her first instinct had been to kill with fire. As she considered that, it disturbed her. That wasn't her. She'd never wish harm on anyone except Torian and his lackeys.

And yet, she had almost taken the man's life without a second thought. Was she being swayed by the dark magic that coursed through her? Or had she changed more than she realized, becoming more like Aimil? She hoped that was not the case.

Venia led them out of the city and along a road that went northeast until they were far enough away that it was unlikely anyone in the city would see them.

"Stand back," she warned.

Gwen and Kalan backpedaled until they were several feet away. Venia closed her eyes and for a moment, nothing happened. Gwen held her breath and watched intently. The change began slowly. Venia's skin lightened until it took on a sickly pale color. She dropped to the ground on all fours, her body wracked with spasms so strong that her arms and legs trembled visibly. Venia hacked loudly. Her shoulder blades protruded from her back and Gwen flinched at how odd it looked.

A loud popping noise filled the air, then her shoulder blades elongated and morphed into wings. Her body lengthened and grew in size until she was easily twenty feet long. Her face extended into a long snout and her skin color changed again, from pale white to silver, and scales took shape all along her form. When it was over, Venia was breathing heavily.

"Does it hurt?" Gwen asked. "When you change, I mean?"

"Yes," Venia replied. "But the more I shift, the less I feel it. The first time I changed, I thought I was going to die."

"Absolutely fascinating," Kalan whispered. "A real dragon. In the flesh."

"Come," Venia said. "Climb onto my back."

Gwen had ridden on her once before, so she had little trouble getting onto Venia's back and settling herself into place. Kalan followed the same path up Venia's shoulder and stood over Gwen.

"Move back," he said.

"Why?"

"So I can sit in the front."

Gwen snorted. "No, you can sit behind me. There's plenty of room." She patted Venia's scales.

"I want the front."

Gwen glared at him and was tempted to pull rank since she was technically the queen, but instead, she shrugged and scooted back, giving him enough room to sit down. Once he was settled, she nudged up behind him.

"You'll want to get a good grip," Gwen said. "Or when she climbs into the air, you'll fall off."

Kalan felt along Venia's neck scales until he found spots that he could grab, then he clenched his hands tightly onto them. Gwen didn't have anything to hold except Kalan. She hesitantly wrapped her arms around his chest and hugged him close. He smelled of lilac, a heady sweet scent, with a touch of vanilla. She thought it odd he smelled so good. It made clinging to him less disagreeable.

Venia dug her claws into the ground and crouched low, poised much like a cat about to pounce. Unlike a cat, however, she sprang into the air and flapped her powerful wings. The air rushed around Gwen like the sound of a raging river and she watched the landscape quickly fade below them. Her stomach churned and her eyes teared from the whipping wind, but she exalted in it all. It wasn't every day she experienced something as miraculous as flying on the back of a dragon.

They flew for a long while and Gwen kept herself occupied by watching the countryside gradually change. The tracts of land were various colors and sizes, and all of them looked small enough that when Gwen held her fingers out, she imagined she could pinch them.

"We're heading down!" Venia roared.

Even though her voice carried, it was still hard for Gwen to hear her clearly over the wind. She leaned forward against Kalan. Venia began her descent and Gwen's stomach lurched again. She doubted she could ever get used to the feeling. They flew low over a wooded area and Venia landed softly in a clearing.

"I must feast," the dragon announced. "There is a town within walking distance if you are hungry. I don't think anyone spotted me, but we should be quick regardless."

Venia lowered herself closer to the ground and Gwen and Kalan slid off her shoulder onto the ground. Gwen felt odd walking on her own legs again, but the feeling was brief.

"I'm famished," Kalan said. "You coming?"

The sight of a dragon eating a deer or some other such animal wasn't an image Gwen wanted in her head. She nodded and they left Venia alone to hunt. The two exited the woods and walked through a wheat field until they reached the road that led to the town. As they drew closer to the boundary of the town, an older man was cutting the wheat down with a scythe while three younger men, whom Gwen assumed were his sons, collected the stocks and tied them into sheaves.

Sweat glistened on their tanned skin and one of the sons paused to offer an admiring stare at Gwen. She waved politely and hoped he wouldn't try to speak to her. He went back to work when one of the others shouted at him for taking a break. Kalan and Gwen entered the town and found a single tavern. It was a small wooden building with a thatched roof. Scrawled beside the door in red paint was the word *Foamy's*.

"A hot meal is calling my name," Kalan said. "And a cold ale."

"Ale sounds good," Gwen agreed.

The two went inside and were greeted with curious stares by the handful of patrons that were scattered across the room. One table, in particular, caught Gwen's attention. Four men in armor bearing Torian's crest were laughing and clinking their tankards together. Gwen's heart skipped a beat, but when the men didn't even look their way, her nerves calmed.

They don't know who I am, she told herself.

Kalan took a seat at a random table and Gwen followed him. Despite the presence of Torian's soldiers, the atmosphere of Foamy's was high spirited. As Gwen listened to the scattered conversations, she assumed the people were all locals. Except for the soldiers. They were minding their own business and the patrons seemed content to ignore their company.

A serving girl sauntered over, her skirt short enough that if she bent down, everything would be revealed. Her top was a loose-fitting piece of white material that barely clung to her ample bosom. Kalan eyed her lustfully and Gwen rolled her eyes at him.

"Typical male," she muttered.

"I'm Poppy," the serving girl said. "What's your fancy?"

"A night with you, Poppy," Kalan said with a not-so-innocent grin.

"Is that so?" Poppy placed her hands onto the table and leaned forward. Gwen watched Kalan's eyes lower to her cleavage.

"Yes indeed."

"Stick around long enough and you just might earn it," Poppy said, straightening. "For now, how does soup sound?"

"That sounds perfect. I want an ale, too."

"I'll take an ale also," Gwen said. "And some bread if you have any that's fresh."

"Coming right up," Poppy said. She strolled away to the kitchen and Gwen waited for Kalan to turn his attention back to her.

"You think we can spend the night?" he asked.

"I hope you're kidding," Gwen replied. "We don't have time for that. Try and keep your mind on what's important, will you?"

"You're no fun," Kalan complained. "Unless you're up for some … strenuous activities?"

"Have you ever been struck by lightning?"

"No," Kalan said confusedly.

"Talk to me like that again and you will be."

Kalan kept his wolfish grin, but Gwen could see the disappointment in his eyes. He shrugged and looked around the room, then set his gaze on the table of soldiers.

"What do you think they're doing here?" he asked.

"Nothing good, I'm sure."

Poppy returned, skillfully holding a bowl of steaming soup in her left hand and two large tankards and a plate of bread with the other. She set them down on the table and "accidentally" dropped a cloth napkin on the floor. Poppy knelt in front of Kalan seductively and peered up at him with a pouty face.

"Woman," Kalan hissed through his teeth. "I'm about to—"

Whatever he said was lost to Gwen's ears as the table of soldiers erupted into raucous laughter and one of them knocked over their tankard, spilling ale onto the table. A stream of golden liquid ran off the edge, splattering onto the floor.

"Poppy!" the drunk soldier shouted. "I need your hands!"

"That's not all you need," another soldier said lewdly.

Poppy rose to her feet and set the napkin in Kalan's lap, pausing with her hand on him for a moment before meandering over to the soldiers. She worked just as seductively with them, crawling on all fours to clean the ale off the floor. Kalan watched jealously.

"You know it's all for show," Gwen said.

"What?" Kalan looked at her, his face flushed.

"The way she's flirting. It's all an act. You do know that?"

"Of course I do," Kalan replied. Gwen knew he was lying.

He ate his meal in silence, but he continuously looked around for Poppy. Gwen sipped her ale, enjoying the familiar atmosphere while holding back the dreaded memory of the night at the Seven Stars where everything had begun.

Kalan finished his meal and downed what remained in his tankard, then walked over to a table of farmers. Gwen watched him curiously but couldn't hear what he was saying. A few of them nodded and looked at Gwen, raising their drinks in salute. Gwen's curiosity turned into suspicion. Was Kalan spreading rumors about her?

He left that table and went to another. Again, the people he spoke with looked at her and offered nods or raised their drinks. Kalan made his way to every table until only the soldiers' remained. As he walked past Poppy, he grabbed a handful of her buttocks and winked at her. He reached the soldiers and leaned down, speaking to the one who'd spilled his drink earlier.

The soldiers laughed at first and Gwen assumed he must have told them a joke. As Kalan continued talking to them, she noticed that their expressions were changing from amusement to glares of anger. Gwen rose from her chair and started walking toward them, intent on grabbing Kalan and heading back to Venia.

One of the soldiers said something, his tone getting louder as he spoke, but all Gwen heard was the word "treason."

"What are you doing?" Gwen demanded, grabbing Kalan by the arm.

"And here she is," Kalan said grandly. "The rightful queen of Isentol's throne!"

The soldiers all stood up at once and Gwen's heart sunk into her stomach. Kalan had betrayed her, just like Aimil had.

"That's enough of your nonsense," the soldier across the table growled. He drew his sword and pointed it toward Kalan.

Kalan looked at Gwen, a brazen look etched on his face. He pulled his arm free of her grasp, grabbed the edge of the table, and flung it into the soldier with the drawn sword.

And then all hell broke loose.

CHAPTER 4

Conal

There was little grumbling during the night as the combined forces of Conal's army moved silently north, hoping to blunt Torian's incursion in time to save what remained of Sorcha's regiment. He was surprised at the determination and speed of the dwarven soldiers keeping pace with the taller human soldiers of Lorkan's army.

In the early hours just before dawn, the forward scouts sent word back that they made contact with Sorcha's rear elements and that Torian's forces had paused their pursuit to lay waste to the city of Blasingdon, allowing her to regroup and break contact with the enemy. Less than an hour later Sorcha strode up to Conal. Her small army, carrying their wounded, flopped down on the side of the road, receiving a welcomed rest.

Sorcha was a handsome tall blond with the strong and fit body of an athlete. She began to drop to her knee when Conal stopped her.

"Are you OK?"

"Yes, m'Lord," she answered, completing the obeisance.

"Don't do that," Conal moaned, bending down to grab her arm and pull her up. "We can all be socially proper at some other time, but not here or now. We have more important things to worry about. What's your status?"

Sorcha brushed the grime from her cheeks, impressed with this prince who seemed unaffected by his position. "We've managed to delay them, but we couldn't do anything to stop them. We were able to break contact when they decided plundering Blasingdon was more important than pursuing us."

"How many?"

Lorkan walked up, nodding respectfully to Conal, "M'Lord," before addressing Sorcha. "I count seventeen walking wounded, six more gravely injured. I've physicians attending them."

"Thank you, my friend," she said, breathing a sigh of relief.

Conal turned to Torgreth. "Tell Storri I need him now."

"Right you are," he grinned and sped off.

"How many able-bodied do you have?" Conal asked Sorcha.

"I started with 757. I'm down to 702 with 32 dead and left behind. We're facing an army three times my size. I've managed to inflict twice my losses on them, but we were in no position to offer combat. I've managed to draw them south, hoping Lorkan would have sufficient forces to counterattack."

"Kilmaryn chose to retain his forces to block any southern probes," Lorkan explained. "Though I didn't like it for it reduces our western attack into Isentol, it makes sense. I pray that he has the good sense to join the battle when it all begins. That said, we number over 7,000."

Sorcha flashed a fierce grin. "More than twice the enemy. It's time for payback."

"Do you know who commands Torian's forces?" Conal asked.

"No, m'Lord. Never got close enough to find out, though I did receive reports of a man of great size who appeared to be commanding. Though interesting, it does not tell me enough to know who it is."

"Do you still have scouts out?"

"Yes, m'Lord, but like all my soldiers, they need rest."

"I've already sent out some scouts to relieve yours," Lorkan said.

"I want to know where they are before we attack," Conal said, stating the obvious. Hands jammed on his hips, he scowled and glanced around. "Where's Drustan?"

"No one has seen him, m'Lord," Lorkan answered.

One of Lorkan's captains strode up with another man who was still catching his breath. "M'Lord, this man has information about the enemy."

At that moment Storri walked up.

"Good. Glad you're here. This scout has just arrived." Conal nodded at the scout. "Go ahead."

The man inhaled a deep breath. "M'Lord, the enemy remains in Blasingdon, continuing to pillage the city."

"Yes," Conal exclaimed with a fist pump. "How long will it take to get to the city?"

"It took me an hour to get here, m'Lord, but I pretty much ran the entire time."

Conal dropped to his knees in the middle of the road. Smoothing out a spot with his hand, he motioned for the others to kneel with him. Drawing a small square in the dirt, he explained, "Here's Blasingdon. Where are the city gates?"

"Here and here," Sorcha pointed to a front and rear gate.

"Have you been in the city?"

"No, m'Lord. We used it as blocking to help us get away."

"No matter. We approach from the south." He drew a line as he talked. "If we assume he's a good commander, he will have patrols even while the city is being ravaged. We need to eliminate any security he has so we can penetrate the city. We do this by dividing our forces to block both gates, dwarves to the main gate, the rest at the back gate. We need to get someone inside the city." He looked up at them. "We find someone who can handle himself and put him in the uniform of the enemy."

"We'll probably need more than one, m'Lord," Storri said, pleased that his army had the main attack through the main gate.

"I agree, General, but it will have to be someone other than a dwarf for obvious reasons."

"I know," Storri nodded.

"We assume that his army is expending their strength in drinking and chasing women —"

"Or men," Sorcha pointed out, self-consciously adding, "We like a good time too."

"Point taken," Conal smiled. "The point is that we want them to be wasted by the time we attack."

"If he's a good commander, he won't allow that," Lorkan countered.

"You are right," Conal replied, "but he *did* stop to allow his soldiers to pillage. That caused him to lose contact with his opponent. Not very smart. The spies we send in will alert us to the right time. When they give the signal, we attack from both sides."

"Challenge and Password?" Sorcha asked.

Conal thought for only a moment. "Challenge is 'Dragon' and password is 'Blood.' Make sure everyone knows it. Dwarves will be easy to recognize as friends. Let's not make any mistakes with the rest of us."

"Questions?"

"Assembly area after the attack?" Lorkan said.

"Operations security?" Storri added.

"Good points," Conal said, standing. "We need three-sixty security. I leave it to you two to coordinate. Suggestions for assembly area?"

"North of the city," Storri suggested.

"Sounds good. Let's get ready to move out. We need volunteers for spy duty."

"What about me, m'Lord?" Sorcha.

"You're in reserve." Seeing her disappointment, he said, "Don't worry. You'll get your turn. Your soldiers are tired and rest." He looked up at the sky that was beginning to lighten. "We got to go." Turning to the others, he said, "Oh, one more thing. I'm going with the spies into Blasingdon."

"What?" Lorkan exploded. "Are you crazy?"

"That's 'are you crazy, m'Lord'," Conal said with a half-smile.

"But… but," Lorkan stammered. "This is madness. You are the overall commander, the king's son. How can we protect you if you go in there?"

"I have stealth skills beyond what anyone else has," he replied.

"It's not a question of skills, my young lord," Storri said, his tone the voice of reason. "We all have no doubt that you can handle yourself. Yet all it takes is one misplaced word, one look of doubt, one misdirected arrow. We can't afford anything happen to you. It would destroy the rebellion. Surely you can see that."

Conal pursed his lips and looked at Voldar. "Well?"

"Really?" Voldar cocked an eyebrow. "You're going to possibly take the wind out of this rebellion because you want to show how stealthy you can be? Do you even have to ask?"

He slowly twisted his head to look at Sorcha who said nothing, merely shaking her head 'no.'

"Fine. You win. I'll be good. But when it comes time to fight, I want a piece of the action."

"If it becomes necessary, my Lord," Lorkan corrected him.

Conal let out an exasperated breath. "Fine."

It was mid-morning by the time they were in position. Lorkan's army had to work its way around the city through the forest. They had dispatched several enemy patrols before they had time to warn of Lorkan's army.

There had been no shortage of volunteers to sneak into the city. Conal settled on ten who donned uniforms from the dead enemy patrols. And there had been plenty of intel provided by fleeing citizens. Tales of rape and murder were the common themes.

Blasingdon itself wasn't a large city, perhaps some three to four thousand residents. Open fields about two furlongs wide separated the city walls from the surrounding forest. But Blasingdon was a fortified city with tall stone walls of grey granite and wide stout oak city gates, which were wide open. Dead bodies, some decapitated others with deep gashes sliced through various parts of their bodies, lay scattered in bloody lumps around the gate and archway across the moat. Several bodies lay where they fell, blocking the doors from being closed. Wisps of smoke near the center of the city curled and dissipated in the morning wind.

It was eerily quiet and Conal impatiently waited for his spies to give the signal, wondering if they had been spotted. Suddenly a man emerged from the rear gates and ran towards them. Lorkan recognized him as did Conal.

"M'Lord," he called out. "It's… it's unreal. They're dead, almost all of them."

"What?" Conal startled. How was it possible ten of his spies could accomplish such results in so short a time?

"We think it's the ale," the spy said, stopping in front of Conal and Lorkan. "We think it's been poisoned. There's still a few alive who are holding out in the center of the city, but for the most part, everyone else is dead. So is their commander."

"Show me," Conal ordered and started back with the spy.

Lorkan quickly issued orders, telling everyone to not drink anything in the city, as he randomly picked a bodyguard of twenty soldiers to protect Conal. "Do the dwarves know yet?"

"Yes, Commander. Heulyn went to tell them."

Conal's bodyguard preceded him through the city gates, stepping over bodies and fanning out and keeping watch.

Conal's mouth gaped open as he saw the multitude of soldiers curled up on the streets, their eyes glazed over in death. He closed his mouth and scrunched his nose at the stench of puke and feces. Stepping over body after body, Conal gaped as he saw their struggle. Some left claw marks on wooden posts or scrapes across the flaking stone walls.

"The last of them are this way, m'Lord," the spy said, directing them around a corner.

To their surprise, a crone of a woman stood in the middle of the street. She was shorter than Korla, due more to her bent of age that actual height. She wore the black of a widow, her silver hair tucked neatly under a black scarf.

"Yer too late," she cackled, her teeth root stained. "Did what I had to. Coulda used yer help yesterday. But now you shows up and late's better'n never."

The bodyguard reacted and began to surround her, weapons ready.

"Leave her alone," Conal commanded and the bodyguards drew back, though still wary. Conal walked up and smiled at her. "Who are you, Mother?"

The woman's head snapped up to stare intently at him. "I know you." She glanced surreptitiously around and lowered her voice. "Yer the Cobra of prophecy. Looks like things're gonna heat up right soon."

Conal looked back over his shoulder at one of the bodyguards. "Fetch Korla." Turning back to the old woman, he smiled kindly at her, waving a hand at the dead soldiers. "So you did all this?"

"Yup." She tapped her nose and winked at him. "Knew they'd start drinkin' when they got here. Stupid soldiers got no discipline. Put poison in the ale. Not all of it, mind you, just the ones I knew they'd start with. Gimme time to do the rest. Slow actin'. Usual takes an hour or two. By then," she sliced a thumb across her throat.

"You've saved us a lot of trouble, Mother," Conal complimented.

"Name's Madlyn." She grinned a root stained smile at him.

"Madlyn," Conal repeated. "How do you know who I am?"

"Oh," she nodded, "I can tell 'cause you got a glow about you, like the one a dragon has."

Conal frowned. "Dragons have a glow about them?"

"Of course, dearie," she maternally replied. "Every living creature has a glow, a color. Some calls it 'Aspect.' Only a few can see it though." She chuckled. "Some spends their lives trying to discover it. It is what it is. Ya can't change it."

Korla walked up, giving the woman a polite smile. "You wanted to see me, m'Lord?"

"M'Lord is it?" Madlyn snickered, then awkwardly bowed. "Fergot my place."

Ignoring the jab, Conal spoke to Korla. "This is Madlyn. She is responsible for this resounding victory."

Lorkan strode up with Storri and Galadyr in tow. "There's no one left, m'Lord." He shook his head in amazement.

"We have a Chronicler with us?" Conal asked.

"Yes, m'Lord."

"Send someone to fetch him. I want Madlyn here to be forever remembered as the Champion of Blasingdon, for it is she who defeated our enemy. I want to make sure it is recorded correctly."

Surprised and flattered, Madlyn blinked in the sudden attention.

"We'll need to toss all the ale —"

"Don't need to," Madlyn interrupted. "Poison's already gone out of it. It don't last. Just long enough to do what I needed."

Conal nodded in understanding then noticed Korla standing to the side, waiting for instructions. "Madlyn, this is Korla. She's a —"

"I know what she is," Madlyn replied. "I could tell it the moment she walked up."

"Because of her As —"

"Association with you, yes," Madlyn interrupted. "Figured you'd have a mage with you."

"Nobody said I was a mage," Korla said, her brows furrowed.

Madlyn grinned at her. "Takes one to know one."

"What? You're a mage?" Korla cocked an eyebrow in disbelief.

Madlyn's smile vanished followed by an intense frown at Korla. "'Course I am." She flipped a hand at the surrounding dead. "How'd ya think I did this?"

"A simple herbalist could have done the same thing," Korla argued.

"Bah." Madlyn turned to Conal. "She may be a looker, but she ain't got the brains to go with it. If yer finished with me, my Lord, I'll go tell the rest of them that escaped that it's safe to come back now."

"Will you come with us?" Conal blurted.

"Pardon?"

"I'm asking you to come with us," Conal said.

Madlyn was again flattered. "Why? I'm just an old woman."

"You're a mage," Conal corrected, "and we can use your help."

"Her?" Korla said, curling a lip. "She's no more a mage than I am a warrior."

Ignoring her, Conal repeated, "Will you come with us?"

"She's an old woman. She'll only slow us down," Korla argued.

Conal help up hand for her to be quiet, though his attention was on the old woman. "Well? Will you come with us?"

Madlyn looked at him then at the indignant Korla before grinning. "I'd love to, m'Lord."

CHAPTER 5

Gwen

"Treason!"

Gwen heard the word reverberate off the walls of the tavern as she watched the guard with the sword crash into the wall. The table bounced off him and struck the floor and broke, sending splinters flying in every direction. The other guards were momentarily surprised, but they quickly recovered their wits and drew their swords. Gwen grabbed onto Kalan's arm again and jerked him back just in time to keep him from being skewered.

"Blasted pigs!" Kalan shouted, trying to break free of her grasp.

"We need to go," Gwen said darkly. She summoned her strength rune and pulled Kalan across the tavern. Two of the guards hurried after them while the other one helped his fallen comrade. Gwen was considering using her fire rune next, but the patrons of the tavern blocked the soldiers and kept them at bay. She spotted Poppy behind the mob. Next to her was an older man who watched the unfolding chaos with an unamused expression.

"I'm sorry!" Gwen shouted, then hurriedly tossed a few coins onto a table and pulled Kalan outside, dragging him along behind her.

"I haven't had this much fun in a long time," Kalan laughed.

"You think almost getting stabbed is fun? I saved your life back there."

"Nah. Even if his blade would have hit me, it would have bounced right off. I've got the steel skin rune."

"The what?"

"If you stop pulling me, I'll show you."

Gwen glanced behind them. The guards hadn't gotten free of the crowd yet, but she doubted it would take much longer. "Show me when we get back to Venia." She released Kalan's arm and the two sprinted until they reached the wheat field, then cut across it and plunged into the woods.

"Venia!" Gwen called out. "We need to move!"

The dragon was in the clearing, her tail flicking back and forth. "What is it?"

"This fool started a fight with some of Torian's soldiers. We need to leave. Now."

Venia lowered herself so they could mount her and then she launched into the air. Gwen was angry at Kalan. What he'd done was stupid and irresponsible. She punched him in the back for good measure, then hissed in pain. Kalan wasn't lying. His skin was hard and her knuckles stung.

"Told you!" he shouted over his shoulder.

Venia's climb through the air plateaued and she continued flying northeast.

"Why did you start a fight with those guards?" Gwen demanded.

"Why not?"

"We have enough problems, and we don't need more. And what did you say to the others? Why did they look at me and raise their drinks?"

"I told them who you were," Kalan replied. "And that we were going to take the fight to Torian."

"Our attack is supposed to be a surprise. Or at the very least, have him looking one way while he gets crushed from the other. If you ever do that again, you'll need more than steel skin for what I have in store for you."

"Is that a threat or a promise?" Kalan teased.

Gwen bit her tongue. Kalan was hotheaded and didn't care if he crossed the line, and arguing with him would accomplish nothing. She avoided speaking to him until they landed. Gwen assumed it was so that Venia could eat again, but as she climbed off the dragon's back and looked around, there was a feeling of familiarity that came over her.

"Where are we?" she asked.

"On the border of Auleavell," Venia answered, glancing around uneasily. She sniffed the air.

"What's wrong?" Gwen also surveyed the area, but she didn't see anything.

"Kirith and his army should be here, but I can't smell them. Unless they are using magic to hide their presence, I don't think they are here yet."

"That's impossible," Gwen said. "Eradore sent word to Kirith before the meeting was over."

"Maybe the message never arrived," Kalan suggested.

"We're in trouble if it didn't." Gwen chewed on her lower lip, thinking. "We need to find Kirith. If his army doesn't march with us to Isentol, we don't stand a chance."

"I'll go," Venia said. "You two stay here. I can fly faster without having to worry about you falling off my back."

Gwen didn't like the idea of waiting around, especially not with Kalan, but it would take her too long on foot. That, and she didn't know where to find the forest-city.

"Go, but please hurry."

Venia sped off, the treetops swaying from the force of her wings. Gwen stared off into the woods. She tried not to think about what would happen if Kirith's forces didn't come through. Without an army to attack from the east, there would be no diversion from Conal's approach.

"Have you heard from your sister?" Gwen asked.

"She tried speaking to me before we left Haddence, but I ignored her."

"You *what?* What if it was something important?"

"I'm sure it wasn't," Kalan replied. "She probably just misses me. We don't separate very often, and when we do, she badgers me for attention. Honestly, it's exhausting. I enjoy getting away from time to time."

"That's fine and well, but next time she reaches out to you, answer her. I need to know what's going on with my brother." Gwen could feel her irritation rising again and she took a deep breath. There was something about

Kalan's attitude that exasperated her to the point of rage.

Gwen paced in circles while they waited for Venia to return. Her nerves eventually calmed and she looked at Kalan. He was sitting on a fallen tree, weaving leaves and thin vines together into a crown. He plucked a white flower and placed it in the center of the crown, then noticed she was staring at him.

"Here," he said, holding out his creation. "I made it for you."

"Is that an apology?" she asked, walking over to accept it.

"Hardly," he laughed. "I don't apologize for being myself."

Gwen looked away, a little embarrassed about her anger towards him. The man was infuriating, true, but maybe she had judged his character incorrectly. She took the crown and set it atop her head.

"How do I look?" she asked.

"Ridiculous," Kalan replied, but he smirked. "If you had pointed ears, you'd look like an elven queen."

"So you aren't always a complete idiot? That's a surprise." Gwen returned his smile. She felt that statement was somewhat true, anyway.

Kalan placed a hand over his heart, a mock look of pain on his face. "You wound me, Your Majesty."

Gwen rolled her eyes. "Show me the rune you mentioned."

Kalan reached down and pulled his pant leg up to reveal a rune that looked like a sword wrapped in ivy. "This one has saved me many times."

"What other runes do you have?" Gwen asked.

"Why? Are you interested in trading magic?"

"Possibly."

"I'll show you mine if you show me yours."

Things like that made Gwen want to punch him in the mouth, but now that she knew it wouldn't even hurt him, she just glared at him instead.

"You're too serious," Kalan said.

"Try having everyone you love be murdered and see how happy you are."

Kalan's smile faded. "I'm sorry," he said. "I didn't know."

"Don't worry about it."

The silence turned awkward and Kalan suddenly pulled off his shirt, revealing several runes in random spots across his chest and even one on his stomach. Gwen didn't have any of them, which made her wonder just how many runes were out there.

"This one unlocks doors," Kalan said, pointing to a rune shaped like a key. Of all places, it was located over his heart. "Spiked ball, wind breath, shield, healing, animal manipulation, telepathic communication," he named them off as he pointed. "And this last one will be a real benefit when we encounter Torian's Prestiges."

Gwen peered closely. The rune looked like an open door. "What does it do?" she asked.

"It absorbs magical attacks."

"That will definitely help." Gwen expected Kalan's body to resemble Aimil's, and she was surprised to find that he didn't have many runes. "Are you searching for more?"

"Not really," Kalan replied, shrugging. "I like what I have." His brow furrowed and he tilted his head curiously. "I don't know how I missed it," he said.

"Missed what?"

"The lines in your eyes. How did you get a dark rune?"

"It's a long story," Gwen said. "I'd rather not talk about it."

"Give me the dark rune and you can have any of mine." His words had an eager tone to them.

"No."

"Just like that, huh? No counteroffer or anything?"

"No," Gwen repeated.

The silence resumed and Gwen went back to pacing. Venia should have been back by now. Had she run into trouble? Were Kirith and his people under attack? Did Torian's arm reach this far? There were too many questions and not enough answers.

"There," Kalan said, shattering her thoughts.

Gwen looked to the sky and saw Venia returning. The dragon swooped down and landed. Kirith was on her back. When he saw Gwen, he leaped off and rushed to her, wrapping her in a hug.

"It is good to see you are well," he said.

"Same here," Gwen replied. "Where's your army? We're marching on Isentol now."

"Now?" Kirith sounded surprised.

"Yes. Did you get Eradore's message?"

"I didn't get anything."

A heavy weight fell onto Gwen's shoulders and she sighed. "I don't know what happened, but we need to go. Conal and his forces are heading for Isentol as we speak. We were to attack from the east and provide a diversion. Now we have a problem."

"I can gather my people, but I will need some time."

"That's the one thing we don't have," Gwen said.

"We'll raise an army on the way," Kalan interjected.

Gwen stared at him incredulously.

"What? You saw how those men responded in the tavern. In a small farming town, they gladly stood up to those guards to help us escape. People are tired of Torian. All they need is a little nudge."

Gwen looked at Kirith.

"He's got a point," the elf said.

Kirith was a male, so of course, he *would* side with Kalan. Gwen looked at Venia questioningly.

"I agree with Kalan," she said. "Kirith's army will come, but not quickly enough. You'll have to convince your people to rise up against Torian."

Gwen thought they were all insane, but it did seem like their only option. "Where's the nearest town?"

"Wespin. It's a few hours from here," Venia said. "If I fly fast enough, we'll cut the time in half."

Gwen looked at each of them. Fate or destiny or possibly death was tightening the rope around her neck, suffocating her. She had to make a decision, but she didn't want to lead innocent men and women to be slaughtered. Conal's words echoed in her mind.

Anyone willing to join us is more than welcome.

"We'll leave our fate in the hands of the people, then," Gwen said. "Kalan, let your sister know what's happened and get me an update from Conal. We need to be in sync now more than ever."

Kalan nodded and stepped away.

"I trust you are still committed to this task?" Gwen asked Kirith.

"You have my oath," Kirith said.

Gwen turned to Venia. "What of the dragons? If there's eleven of you left, where are the others?"

"They're heading to Isentol," Venia answered.

That fact gave Gwen some solace, at least.

"We've got another problem," Kalan said. "Korla says that Conal and his army are attacking a city called Blasingdon because Torian's army has crossed the border into Tir Manach."

"It's one thing after another," Gwen complained. "Can you use your telepathy rune to contact other mages?"

"It depends on how far away they are," Kalan replied. "And I need to know their name or their general location."

"The Great Library is where she should be. Her name is Marjorie."

"I'll see what I can do." Kalan sat on the ground and closed his eyes.

"I hate to leave you with this situation, but I must gather my people. We will meet you in Isentol, Solara willing."

"I understand," Gwen said. "Maybe we'll stay alive long enough to see you again."

Kirith bowed his head and left, sprinting into the woods. Gwen watched Kalan, occasionally glancing at Venia. The dragon remained quiet but returned her gaze. Finally, Kalan's eyes opened and he stood.

"Marjorie says a force of Prestiges left the Great Library already and are headed to Isentol. She's going to tell them to meet us in Wespin."

"Thank the gods," Gwen said. "At least we have magic to battle magic."

"We should make haste," Venia said. "The faster you can spread word of the coming battle, the more people will join our cause."

Gwen motioned for Kalan to mount Venia first, but he shook his head. "Take the lead," he said. Gwen did so and Kalan sat behind her.

"Hold on tight," Venia said, then launched into the air.

Once they were gone, Aimil stepped out from the trees. She watched them fade in the distance and then opened the letter Eradore had penned. She'd intercepted the message hawk by accident while magically teleporting to Auleavell. Aimil read over it again, then tossed the parchment aside and activated her rune.

It was time to cut the head off the snake.

CHAPTER 6

Conal

While Lorkan and Storri sent scouts out patrol the surrounding area, ensuring none of the enemy had escaped, Conal, the two mages, his battle captains, and bodyguards set out to find the enemy commander. As they made their way through the streets Madlyn caught up to Korla, grinning confidently at her.

"Don't worry, dearie, I won't steal your man away from you."

"He's not my man," she huffed, "and even if he was, I doubt you would be a threat."

"Ooh, sure of ourselves, are we?" She smirked at her.

Korla stiffened. "I don't know why he wants to bring you along. I can handle it."

"Like how you helped when he attacked the city?" She parried with a feigned innocent grin.

"He didn't need my help," Korla tartly replied.

"Of course he didn't," she chuckled. "I'd already helped him."

Pursing her lips, Korla picked up her pace to catch up to Conal.

Conal was having second thoughts about inviting the old woman, but she was resourceful and he needed a mage, someone unafraid to do what is necessary. That she seemed to enjoy picking on Korla might be a problem. He'd wait and see. Still, having two mages with him was more than he had expected.

They found the commander slouched in an imposing chair set on a platform in the reception room of the burgomaster's residence hall. His hands draped over the arm rests, a spilled drinking horn on the floor by his feet. The eyes, glazed over in death, stared at the far wall.

Conal was the first to notice it, a beautifully cut obsidian stone set in gold filigree on a necklace chain dangling from his neck. Reaching for it, he startled when Madlyn slapped his hand away, placing her other hand between him and the stone.

"You don't wants to do that, young Lord," she warned, "if you don't wants him to know yer here."

"Why?"

"Don't touch it," Madlyn commanded, glancing around the room. Retrieving a cloth napkin on a bureau by the wall, she wrapped the stone inside the cloth before casting a look back at Korla. "Go ahead. Tell 'im."

"Tell him what?" Korla replied confused.

"About the stone," Madlyn prompted.

"What about the stone?"

Madlyn frowned at her. "You sure yer a mage?"

"Yes," came the indignant reply.

"Enough," Conal interjected. "Why don't *you* tell me, Madlyn?"

Casting a suspicious look at Korla, Madlyn explained as she pulled the necklace over the dead man's head, "It's a Linking Stone."

"Linking stone?" Conal and Korla said in unison.

"Yes." She gave Korla a look of disappointment. "You have much to learn, dearie."

"I'm not your dearie," Korla shot back.

"Just stop," Conal commanded. "What does a linking stone do?"

"It's a connection, young Lord, between two people; usual a mage or wizard is at one end. The man holds the stone like this," she held the cloth in her hand, "and when he does, it tells the mage that he is ready to talk."

"How? They're too far apart," Lorkan said.

"That's why it's called 'magic,' dearie," she replied with a twinkle. "Once the connection is made, the mage then commands the man to do his bidding. If the mage is strong enough, he can use the man's eyes to see what he sees."

"By the gods," Storri snarled.

"No, dearie," she smiled with only her lips. "The gods got nothin' to do with this."

"What should we do with it?" Lorkan asked, shifting a worried look between the old woman and Conal.

Conal knitted his brow in thought. "Can the mage be fooled? I mean, supposed someone took the stone and pretended to be the commander. Could the mage be fooled into thinking he was still controlling the commander?"

Madlyn's eyes widened. "I know whatcher thinkin' young Lord."

"Answer the question."

Madlyn paused. "Yes. It is possible. But… it'll work only as long as the mage believes he has the right man. Pray that the mage is distracted for he can plump the depths of the pretender's mind. If the mage discovers the deceit, the pretender is as good as dead for the mage with destroy him... from the inside out."

Conal nodded, inhaling a deep breath. "Where is the tallest building in the city?"

"We're in it," Lorkan said. "Remember? We saw the tower above the walls."

"Good." Conal turned to eh dwarven commander. "Storri, I need you to hide your army so that no dwarves can be seen."

"What're you gonna do?"

"I have a plan," he answered. "Lorkan. You take your army and assemble them outside the main city gates."

"What are you going to do, m'Lord?" Lorkan asked, his concern obvious.

"Gonna have a little chat with a certain mage," he replied.

"No," Korla burst. "You're crazy."

Conal's face hardened and he jabbed a finger at her. "You and Madlyn are with me. The rest of you, go do what I asked." Glaring at the bodyguard, he commanded, "And you all stay here."

"Are you sure you wants to do this, young Lord?" Madlyn peered intently at him.

"No, I'm not sure, but I have an idea and I have to try. Now please, we're wasting time."

"But, m'Lord –"

"No 'buts' Lorkan. I know what I'm doing."

"Do you?" Korla sharply replied.

"You go with General Storri and stay out of the way," he snapped, immediately regretting his anger when he saw the hurt in her eyes.

Madlyn led the way through the burgomaster's citadel. "Been here often enough. Always wondered what the view was like at the top."

Conal opened the door for her, letting her slowly lead the way up the spiraling stairs. Though chaffing to get to the top, he calmed himself, praying that his gambit worked.

"Anything I should know about working the stone?"

She paused on the step above him to look over her shoulder at him. "It is dangerous what you plan to do. If it works, fine. If not…" She shrugged. Resuming the climb up, she said, "Hold the stone loose in yer hands, just the fingers touching it. That way if he discovers who you are, it's easier to drop the stone. Tell him what he wants to hear. Butter 'im up real good, but don't overdo it. Remember who yer supposed to be."

She pushed through the door at the top of the stairs and stepped out onto the narrow walkway around the spire.

Conal stepped out behind her, immediately feeling vertigo causing him to firmly grasp the iron railing.

"Are you OK?"

"Yes… yes." He swallowed and forced himself to relax as he gazed out over the city walls to the forest in the distance then down at the streets littered with bodies.

"You sure you want to do this?" She gave him a hard stare.

"Yes," he resolutely answered.

Unwrapping the stone, she slipped it over his head, careful not to touch the stone. "Touch the stone with just the fingers of yer left hand. The mage will know your there."

Obeying, Conal touched the stone and felt an immediate tingle up the arm, into his shoulder and up his neck and into his head. His vision clouded to almost black. Then a voice spoke inside his head.

What? Ah, there you are. Where have you been?

I… I'm where I'm supposed to be, Conal replied.

Don't get smart with me. Did you do what I asked?

Conal paused trying to think of the right answer.

What's wrong with you?

Conal forced himself to relax, calling in the deception skills he learned as a highwayman. *I'm a little drunk,* he giggled.

Drunk? Where are you? the voice snarled.

Blasingdon.

Did you destroy the city?

Of course.

Let me see?

Conal bent his head to stare down at the streets. The weird feeling of someone else using his eyes sent a shiver up his spine.

Good, good. Yes. Stop. I see uniforms. Who are they?

They're the ones I been chasing. Managed to corner them in the city here.

Where are your soldiers?

Outside the town. Conal lifted his eyes to stare off in the distance beyond the city walls.

Why?

All the ale's gone. Conal snorted a laugh

Don't be a fool. I didn't send you here to lay around getting drunk.

My soldiers needed a break. Besides, the ale was free and so were the women. He snickered, conjuring up an image of woman he had met a year ago, hoping the vision would be convincing.

Focus, damn you. You're wasting time.

What's the rush?

Are you that stupid? I chose you because you were useful. Don't make me regret my decision.

Conal felt a flash of intense pain explode in his head. "Ow. OK, OK. I'm sorry."

Are you finished in Blasingdon?

Yes.

Then get moving.

Uh... Where am I going?

Has the ale befuddled you that much?

Conal felt the rising irritation in the voice. He needed to be cautious.

I... I am a little disoriented –

Disoriented? Now there's an interesting word. I'm surprised you were able to use it in a sentence.

Conal silently berated himself for forgetting who he was pretending to be. *I'm not stupid,* he indignantly replied.

Of course you aren't, the mage said with not so subtle sarcasm. *Calm yourself Firyn. You still have work to do. Go north. Hafgan waits for you. You will join her and attack Gorwick. I want that city destroyed. Let me know when you have succeeded.*

Which one of us commands? Conal demanded as though affronted he was not specifically named in charge.

The mage chuckled. *Vanity, vanity. Does it matter? She is a proven leader.*

So am I, Conal huffed. *Why must I submit to a woman? I didn't need her help laying waste to Blasingdon.*

I will acquiesce to your request… this time. Do not try my patience again.

Yes Master.

That's better. Say it again.

Yes, Master.

One more time. The mage sniffed a laugh of derision

"Yes Master," Conal droned, feeling an intense lethargy permeate his body.

Laying the clothe over her hand, Madlyn snatched the stone with one hand and slapped him across the face with the other.

"Yeow," he startled, a hand at his cheek. "What was that for?"

"You were starting to lose yourself."

"What do you mean?"

"The mage was beginning to exert control over you."

"How did you know?"

Madlyn peered intently into his eyes, examining them, finally nodding. "Yer fine now. I could tell by the voice you used at the end, like someone drugged. Well? Did you discover what you wanted?"

"Yes," Conal replied, reasonably sure he didn't want to try that experiment again. "The dead commander below is named Firyn."

Madlyn cocked an eyebrow at him. "I coulda told you that. You didn't need to do this." She held up the cloth wrapped around the stone.

"And I also learned that Firyn is on his way north to join Hafgan and attack Gorwick."

Madlyn grinned at him. "I didn't know that. What are we gonna do?"

"We're going to head north," he replied. He started to turn then abruptly stopped. "Who do you think was the mage at the other end?"

"Can't be sure," she thoughtfully replied. "Few mages got that power. My guess it was probably Grimmar. You were lucky this time. Don't think ya oughta try it again."

"Not a problem," Conal agreed. "C'mon. I need to tell the others."

Twenty minutes later, he stood in the middle of the armies with Madlyn, Lorkan, Storri, Galadyr, and Korla whose insolent look told him she wasn't happy. Voldar and Torgreth, though not formally invited, stood at the edge of the group. Conal smiled at them and motioned them closer.

"The enemy here is supposed to be heading north to join forces with a woman commander named Hafgan for an attack on Gorwick. We will head north to join them."

"We're gonna attack Gorwick?" Torgreth blurted.

"No, my friend. We're going to destroy Hafgan and her army. I have an idea. It's going to require us making her believe we are Firyn's army come help her. Once we destroy her army, we head into Isentol. It's about time Torian learns he is not in control like he thinks he is."

"Easier said than done," Storri commented. "What's your plan?"

"We'll need scouts well out in front so that she doesn't know who we are. The scouts, when confronted will need to play the part of Firyn's loyal soldiers. She won't suspect anything if she believes we are who she thinks we are."

"I like it," Lorkan nodded. "Gives us a chance to assess and deploy.

"We don't know how big her army is," Storri pointed out.

"I know," Conal agreed, "but, surprise is always to our advantage. Besides, we have two powerful mages with us."

While Madlyn preened, Korla's insolence vanished, replaced by a sudden feeling of overwhelming inadequacy.

CHAPTER 7

Gwen

"Tell me again how this is going to work?" Gwen asked. She rubbed the back of her neck, trying to work out the soreness.

"We'll spread the word in the streets," Kalan replied. "Anyone you see is a potential ally."

"Won't that draw the attention of Torian's soldiers?"

"Probably, but unless you have a better idea, I think it's worth the risk."

Gwen knew Kalan was right, but she still didn't like it. She also didn't like being forced to change their strategy at the last minute. With a city as large as Wespin, there were bound to be problems they couldn't account for.

They had arrived less than an hour ago and were waiting near a well for Venia to meet them in her elven form. From the air, Gwen had seen that Wespin was shaped like a compass, with the city divided into four smaller sections by large waterways that dispersed water from the nearby river into the city.

"There's only three of us," Gwen lamented. "We could cover more ground if we had more bodies."

"And if a bard had four arms, he could play two instruments. What's your point? Focusing on the problem doesn't get us anywhere."

Gwen looked at Kalan and he held his hands up placatingly. "I'm just saying, we should find the silver lining, no matter how thin it is."

"I know, but it's difficult," Gwen replied.

"Nothing of value is ever easy," Kalan said.

"You seem too young to have experienced many difficulties."

Kalan laughed. "You haven't met my father. He forces difficulty on me constantly."

"I'm sorry."

"Don't be. Maybe once this is all over, I'll be considered a hero and can choose my own path."

"What do you mean?" Gwen asked.

"I don't want to be a mage. Were it up to me, I would live by the sword, carving out glory and fame with my skill."

Gwen was surprised. Kalan was more like her in that regard. When Eradore had first told her she was a mage, she didn't want to walk that path. Yet, she had been forced upon it and walked it even now, unsure of what life would be like without magic. Lyra came into view at the end of the street and she joined them at the well.

"We should split up to cover more ground," she said.

"I don't think we should," Gwen replied. "What if one of us gets into trouble? The others wouldn't know."

"Normally, I would agree with Lyra," Kalan said. "But in this instance, I must side with Gwen. We don't have enough people as it is. If one of us were to get caught by the guards, it would be impossible to free them. We should stick together."

Lyra frowned, but she acquiesced. "Very well."

Gwen waited for one of them to decide where to start, but they were both staring at her.

"What are we waiting for, Your Majesty?" Kalan asked.

"Stop calling me that," Gwen huffed. "It's just Gwen." She looked around at the various shops that lined the street, thinking. And then an idea came to her. "We could find bards to help spread the message."

"With what money?" Kalan frowned.

"The money Eradore gave me. It should be plenty to convince those greedy minstrels to sing of our plight."

"And how will we eat?"

"Do you want food, or do you want to save our kingdom?"

"I'd like both, and I don't want to be forced to choose."

"Too bad," Gwen said.

They navigated the crisscrossing streets until they found a tavern that had music playing within. Gwen handed Kalan a handful of coins.

"See what you can do," she said.

He shrugged and entered the tavern. Lyra and Gwen waited outside. After a few moments of uncertainty, Kalan returned with a smile.

"That was easy. The man probably would have done it for free."

Gwen doubted that, but she was happy regardless. "Start telling everyone we need their help. When we find places like this," she pointed at the tavern, "or come across bards on the street, we give them some money and keep going."

The three of them spread out across the street and began stopping passerby. Initially, Gwen found some resistance. People thought she was a beggar who wanted a handout, but when she started talking, they listened with rapt attention. Kalan had been right— people *were* tired of Torian.

Gwen expected their task to take them most of the day, but as they spread through the city, so too did their words. By the time they crossed the bridge into the second section of the city, people were already aware of their message and were spreading it themselves.

"We told people who are interested to meet us outside the city, but we don't have anywhere to host them. We've no tents or bedrolls or anything," Kalan said.

"I thought about that," Gwen replied. "These people live here. They can sleep in their homes until we are ready to march."

"When will that be?" Lyra asked.

"Hopefully at dawn's fight light, but we can't leave until the Prestiges from the Great Library arrive. They are the key to battling Torian's."

"What if they aren't here by then?"

Gwen didn't even want to consider that as an outcome, but it was possible. "Then we go ahead without them and leave them a message to continue to

Isentol. Whether we have five people or five hundred doesn't matter now. We just have to get there and get Torian's attention before he focuses his might on Conal and his army."

"Five hundred would get his attention more than five," Kalan said with a chuckle. "Imagine five people showing up outside the castle gates demanding he abdicate the throne. I don't think he'd even notice."

Gwen couldn't help but smile. The sight would indeed be laughable. A commotion nearby caught their attention and Gwen spotted a contingent of soldiers harassing a young boy.

"Vengeance is coming!" the boy shouted as the guards tried to wrangle him under control.

"It looks like they've heard their days are numbered," Kalan said.

Gwen had considered the fact that she or Kalan could get arrested, but she *hadn't* considered that the soldiers might target innocent people. Before she could decide what to do, Kalan rushed to join the fray. He lowered his shoulder and drove it into the back of one soldier, sending him crashing to the ground.

Kalan turned to the next one and grabbed onto his helmet, forcing the soldier's head down onto his knee. The armor clanged as if it had struck a shield and the soldier cried out in pain as Kalan tossed him aside. Gwen blinked several times before breaking out of her reverie. She sprinted to the boy.

"Are you all right?" she asked.

"I am now," he said with a large smile. "Pummel him, sir! Show that pig what for!"

"You should get home," Gwen said. "It's too dangerous for you out here."

The boy looked like he was going to argue, then nodded and ran off. Gwen turned around in time to see Kalan take down another soldier. Within a matter of seconds, he had subdued three of them. The remaining two had drawn their swords, but they were keeping their distance and seemed hesitant to engage Kalan.

"Tell your fellows that if they harass anyone else, the wrath of Her Majesty Queen Gwen will find them!" Kalan shouted.

A bell started ringing a few buildings down and Gwen realized they were near a guard outpost. She cursed under her breath.

"We need to hide somewhere," she said to Kalan. Before she'd finished her sentence, she spotted soldiers bolting out of the building. Someone met with the soldiers and pointed in her direction. Gwen squinted to see who it was. Why would one of the citizens rat them out? As she stared, it almost looked like …

"No," Gwen said. "It can't be."

"What is it?"

"More guards," she replied. "And a powerful enemy. A mage."

"We can take him," Kalan said with a tone of superiority.

"It's a her, and I don't know about that. She's got more runes than most prostitutes body counts."

Kalan gave her an odd look and she shrugged in response. The soldiers started running toward them.

"Here they come!" Gwen turned to Lyra. "Hide!"

"I'm tired of hiding," Lyra replied. "I want blood."

The tone of her voice sent a shiver along Gwen's spine. She nodded. The time for running was over. It was time to fight. Lyra issued a roar as she partially shifted into a dragon. Her body stretched and changed, but only until she looked like a massive lizard. She charged the two soldiers who'd been keeping their distance and whacked one with her tail. The other one she snapped up in her jaws, crunching the man's bones loudly. Gwen blanched and turned to face the approaching soldiers. She held up her right hand and inhaled a deep breath, then summoned the magic of her fire rune.

"*Tine,*" she said, speaking the rune's name.

A wave of flames erupted from her palm and shot forth, engulfing the nearing soldier. He screamed in terror and anguish, his armor melting under the intense heat. He was the first to die. Gwen spoke the rune again, killing another soldier. She watched as more of them came out of the outpost, and she watched them as they died, writhing in the wrath of her fire.

"Watch this!" Kalan shouted.

She kept her focus on the magic but offered a glance in his direction. He was pointing to the sky where a group of birds wheeled overhead. He spoke a word and the birds changed direction, diving down to attack the guards.

"That's nothing!" Gwen shouted back. She cut off the magic and switched hands. "*Tintreach.*"

Lightning flashed from her fingertips and forked apart, striking two soldiers simultaneously. They died instantly and the bolts ricocheted, killing two more soldiers. Despite their magical attacks, the soldiers kept coming at them.

"Amateur!" Kalan laughed.

He spun in a circle and held his right hand out, shouting another word. This time, an ethereal ball formed. He threw it at the center of a small group of soldiers. The ball grew as it sped through the air. It landed on the ground, quivered briefly, and then exploded, sending hundreds of spikes airborne.

"That's impressive," Gwen said. "But not as impressive as this!"

She called on the magic of the might rune and waited until a soldier was right on top of her before she punched him in the chest plate as she yelled, "*Láidreacht!*"

The armor caved in under her enhanced blow, crushing the man's chest and sending him reeling. Gwen was just as surprised as Kalan. They continued in the sordid game, pushing each other into more insane ways of taking out their enemies until the street was littered with dead soldiers and none remained. Lyra stalked around like a predator, her head swiveling as she looked for more enemies. The general citizenry had cleared the area already, and as Gwen surveyed their work, she started to feel ill.

She had killed many people, and she had laughed doing it. Bile rose in her throat and she forced it down, gathering her saliva and swallowing it to ease the burning of her tonsils. Their fight wasn't over, though.

Bells were ringing all around the city. More guards would be coming, but Gwen wasn't thinking about that. She watched Aimil slowly approach, their gazes fixed on one another.

"I see you've learned some new tricks," Aimil said, casting a glance at the bodies.

"Why are you here?" Gwen asked, clenching her fists. Aimil's betrayal burned in her veins like her fire rune and Gwen wanted nothing more than to obliterate the woman from existence.

"I'm here to kill you," Aimil replied casually. "Torian tires of the rebellion and he's about to stamp the life out of it."

"He can try, but his cruelty lacks our passion. We *will* defeat him."

"Enough talk," Aimil spat, then she swept her arm up and a rush of air struck Gwen, pushing her back a few feet.

Kalan turned her magic against her, using his wind breath rune to turn the direction of the gale back at her. She dove out of the way, rolling aside and coming back up quickly. Her body rippled and suddenly there were five of her, each one identical to the others. Gwen couldn't tell which one was the real Aimil. She spoke the name of the lightning rune, shattering one of the illusions into pieces like broken glass.

The other four scattered and hurled different spells at Gwen and Kalan, putting them on the defensive. A faint blue glow appeared around Kalan and Aimil's attacks bounced off harmlessly. He threw another spiked ball and closed the distance between himself and Gwen, sharing his shield with her. The ball exploded and destroyed two of the four illusions while also sending a wave of spikes into the surrounding buildings. Gwen was glad the area had been evacuated. The devastation the spikes caused would have killed many innocent people.

Aimil knelt and dug her fingers into the dirt between the cobblestones of the street. The ground shook around Gwen and Kalan before a gaping hole opened up, threatening to swallow them. Gwen wrapped her arms around Kalan and summoned the might rune, throwing them backward and away from the hole.

"I think you were right," Kalan said as they got back on their feet. "She's a worthy opponent." He paused. "We might want to run."

"We can't. She'll find us. Aimil won't stop until she's dead. Or we are."

"Then we need to find a way to kill her," Kalan said, stating the obvious.

"I'm open to ideas."

When Kalan didn't offer any, Gwen looked at him. He shrugged. "I can shield us and we can try to get close to her. That's all I've got."

Gwen considered each of her runes. The healing and life rune were obviously no good in this fight. "That might work," Gwen finally said. "If we can get close enough, I can use my dark rune."

"What does it do?"

"It steals life, but I have to be touching her."

"So we have to get *really* close," Kalan said.

"Too close," Gwen replied. "There's no telling what other magic she's got."

"What if we had a diversion?"

"Such as what?"

Kalan tilted his head and Gwen looked in the direction he was hinting at. Lyra was perched atop the roof of a building near Aimil, her reptilian eyes watching the woman intently.

"She must know Lyra's there," Gwen said. "She's been watching the whole time."

"Maybe, but a diversion doesn't have to be a surprise. It just has to draw her attention."

"Can you communicate with Lyra and tell her what we're doing?"

"I don't know if it works with dragons, but I can try." He closed his eyes.

Gwen watched Lyra, but if the dragon could feel Kalan's mind, her demeanor didn't show it.

"She'll pounce on her," Kalan said. "And it was surprisingly easy to touch her mind. Even more than with Korla."

Gwen didn't care about that, but she smiled anyway. Lyra leaped off the building and Aimil immediately turned to face her.

"Hold on!" Gwen shouted and grabbed Kalan's hand. She summoned the runes on her thighs, only a vague idea of what they did as she said, *"Luas."*

They sped forward so quickly that everything around them blurred. Gwen barely stopped in time before they passed Aimil completely. Lyra landed beside them, her jaws snapping at Aimil, but the woman easily sidestepped out of Lyra's path. Gwen reached out as her speed slowed and latched onto Aimil's arm, jerking her and Kalan forward roughly before coming to a stop. With vengeance within her reach, Gwen fell into the power of the dark rune.

"Draein saoil."

Aimil screamed in anger and pain as her lifeforce was violently ripped away. Gwen felt the energy streaming into her own body, addictive and powerful. It revitalized her flagging strength and she could feel Aimil weakening. Despite the euphoria, Gwen knew the magic was unholy. It was magic so dark, no one should ever have discovered it. Aimil dropped to her knees and her face looked like it had aged several years within just a few seconds.

It's wrong, her subconscious told her.

Yet it felt so good. Aimil deserved to die. She'd poisoned many elves and some of them had died. This was the fate she deserved, to suffer and die painfully. And yet, there was a fate that could be worse for the woman. An idea struck Gwen and she focused on the stream of life energy flowing out of Aimil. She followed the trail until she found what she was looking for. A glowing sphere of golden light hovered near Aimil's spine. Gwen turned the power of the dark rune on it and with a single thought, she snuffed the light out.

Aimil's *bunús* died, and with it, her access to magic.

CHAPTER 8

Conal

For two days, Conal's army swarmed north, moving as quickly as possible, yet not so fast as to tire. He spent most of the time either with Lorkan or Storri discussing battle plans and listening to their counsel based upon years of experience. Of especial concern was remaining unnoticed for as long as possible. Scouts had been deployed well to their front and flanks to provided early warning. Likewise, Conal had the two mages pay attention to the skies for messenger birds.

Korla wasn't especially happy to be relegated to birdwatching and decided to check in with Kalan only to have to listen to his boastful exploits of getting to ride a dragon and some adventure in a pub where he threw a table at some of Torian's soldiers. The way he told it, he was having the time of his life.

And here she was, bored, playing second fiddle to some old woman and looking for birds. Conal frustrated her. Why couldn't he see that she was far more valuable than merely birdwatching or checking to see what Gwen was doing. She was a mage, a powerful mage and when the time came, she would show him.

But it was more than that. Ever since he told her to call him Conal and she had politely reminded him that he was a lord and she was a mage, he became distant, almost brusque, especially when that woman showed up claiming to be a mage.

As if reading her thoughts, Madlyn sidled up next to her and spread her lips in a root stained smile. "Don't worry dearie. Yer secret's safe with me."

"What secret," Korla coldly replied.

"That yer new at this mage business. Just started have you?"

Korla glared at her. "I was born to be a mage."

Madlyn barked a laugh, shook her head, and dropped back so that Korla rode alone, stewing at the insult.

Riding behind them, Conal saw the exchange, wondering why the old woman was picking in Korla. He was tempted to ride up beside her but didn't want to have to deal with her moods.

Madlyn dropped back far enough to ride alongside Conal. "Relax, young Lord," she grinned. "I know what I'm doing. Up 'til now, all her training's been schoolin'. Never had to kill a man, don't know what it's like to take a man's life, and don't know what it's like to lose her family. She's unsure of herself. Just makin' sure when the time comes, she'll be ready."

"By picking on her?" He looked at Korla whose sour expression hadn't changed.

"It's what she needs," she said with a shrug. "You'll see."

Unconvinced, Conal was about to question her teaching methods when he noticed a rider approaching. The man circled around Conal and reined in his horse to ride beside him.

"Forward scouts have made contact, m'Lord. Per your instructions, two scouts have ridden into the enemy's camp to report to the enemy commander."

"Good work," Conal complimented, his worry increasing. Everything depended on Hafgan believing they were Firyn's army. "Go back to your position."

"Yes, m'Lord."

Before the rider had spurred his mount forward, Conal turned to Voldar. "Tell Storri we're stopping. I want to hear what the enemy commander has to say before we get much closer, but he needs to be prepared in case we have to attack."

As Voldar sped off, Conal issued the same instructions to another courier and sent him ahead to Lorkan. Ten minutes later, both Storri and Lorkan came riding up.

"Once the scouts have returned, we'll know how to position," Conal said.

"It's a dangerous game we play, m'Lord," Lorkan said. "I pray my scouts are not betrayed."

"I know," Conal fretted and for the next hour, nervously waited for the two scouts to return, occasionally looking up the scattered billowy clouds in the early afternoon sky. Every now and then he thought he saw a hawk and would shoot a glance at the two mages whose lack of interest told him not to worry.

Storri and Lorkan had returned to their armies to reposition security in anticipation. It was with great relief when Lorkan returned with the two scouts.

"What news?" Conal asked, his eyes bright with excitement.

"It was a piece of cake, m'Lord," the one scout said. He was a wiry man with russet hair and beard. "We rode in like we were glad to finally be there. They took us to the commander straight away. She's a tall one, strong and demanding. She started to interrogate us a bit, asking where the rest of us were."

"But we acted the part," the other scout added. She was the same height as the man, sinewy with auburn hair. "I greeted her and said that Commander Firyn sends his respects and asks where she wanted him to position his forces. That seemed to flatter her. My impression was that she wasn't keen on him being there."

"They've got the city under siege," the man explained, "but they're spread thin. They've concentrated most of their forces at the main gates."

"They were halfway finished building a battering ram," the woman said, "when we left, and positioning catapults."

"Could you tell the size of her forces?" Conal asked.

The two scouts exchanged a look before the woman spoke. "From what we could tell, m'Lord, they were less than half what we got."

"Yes," Conal exclaimed.

"Look who I found wandering around," Storri called out riding up, Drustan and a woman of aristocratic bearing riding beside him.

"Drustan," Conal declared. "Where have you been? You've missed all the excitement."

"Good to see you too, my Lord," he replied with a smile.

"Since when have you been so formal?" Conal gently chided.

Drustan shrugged. "You are who you are. M'Lord, this is Meinir, a half-druid like me. I have been absent due to discovering her whereabouts. When I explained who you are and what you were doing, she insisted on helping."

Conal immediately understood, greatly pleased. "You are most welcome, Meinir."

"Thank you, my Lord," she respectfully answered. Meinir was a comely woman with long raven black hair that cascaded down her shoulders and contrasted sharply with her milk-white skin. She wore the raiment of a huntress: brown leather breeches tucked in darker brown boots, a forest green v-neck, short sleeved top of finely woven cotton, and a thin gold circlet holding her hair back. Two crossbows dangled from the pommel of her saddle.

"So, what's your plan?" Drustan asked.

"Meinir," Madlyn exclaimed riding up. "By the gods, it's wonderful to see you again."

"And you too, Madlyn," she replied with a warm smile. Turning to Conal, she added, "You are indeed fortunate to have a mage with her powers with you."

"We have another," Conal quickly pointed out as Korla eased her mount into the mix.

"So I see," Meinir noncommittally answered, causing Korla to grimace.

"What *is* your plan?" Drustan repeated.

"We infiltrate and attack them from the inside," Conal confidently replied. Seeing the confused looks on the newcomers' faces, he explained, "Their commander thinks we're the forces of her compatriot from down in Blasingdon come here to help her attack Gorwick, which she presently has under siege. Lorkan and his army will move into the enemy camp and pretend to set up bivouac. Meanwhile, Storri's forces will position themselves to attack from the opposite direction."

"Would you like our help?" Meinir asked.

"Absolutely," Conal said before seeing Drustan's tight lips. "That is, if you'd like to. I trust you to best place yourselves where needed."

"Thank you," Drustan nodded, giving Meinir a look of irritation.

"What about us," Madlyn spoke up, "the young'un and me?"

"I'm not a 'young'un'," Korla snapped.

"We don't know if she has mages with her," Conal hastily said, "so I'll need you both to be on the lookout for anything strange. You know best how to deal with that." Looking pointedly at Korla, he said, "Listen to her and do what she says."

"What?" Korla stiffened, her nostrils flaring. "I'll not —"

"Yes you will," Conal growled. "Either that or go back and find that brother of yours with Gwen." Dismissing her from his attention, he turned to the others. "Time to get ready."

While Storri positioned the dwarven army to the east of the city, Lorkan and his soldiers moved up the main road toward Gorwick. Conal and Lorkan placed themselves towards the rear of the army, with the plan of getting as much of his army in position before the deception was discovered. Conal searched for Drustan and Meinir but no one knew where they were.

Much to Conal's surprise and advantage, Hafgan was preoccupied with placing the catapults and berating those constructing the battering ram that she didn't want to be bothered with the new arrivals, expecting Firyn to come to her. It was a battle of personalities as she expected to be the overall commander. Yet when Firyn failed to show up, she sent someone to look for him.

Conal was in conversation with Lorkan when Hafgan's emissary arrived, haughty as his commander. The emissary, a plump staff officer who flaunted his position, rode up and flashed a condescending glance at Conal and Lorkan. "Where's Firyn?" The man arched his back and cast a slow regal glance at the surrounding bivouac.

"He's not here," Conal indifferently replied.

"Well where is he?" the emissary tersely demanded.

Scratching his head, Conal frowned at Lorkan. "I'm confused. Was it my turn or yours to watch him today?"

Lorkan shook his head. "Y'know, I'm not sure. Tell you what, I'll flip you for it." He reached into his pocket and pulled out a coin. "Heads is my turn, tails is yours."

"Two out of three?" Conal grinned.

"Two out of three it is."

Lorkan had no sooner flipped the coin in the air when the emissary barked, "By the gods, what is wrong with you two? Do you know who I am?"

As Lorkan caught the coin and smacked it on the back of his hand, Conal stared intently at the man, shook his head and turned to Lorkan. "Well?"

Lorkan removed his hand and sighed. "Heads. Advantage yours." He flipped the coin again.

"Did you hear what I said?" the emissary snapped.

Conal raised a hand at him to be quiet though his attention was on the coin on the back of Lorkan's hand. "Hold on."

"Tails," Lorkan triumphantly announced.

Conal swiveled his head to grin at the emissary. "One more tells the tale. Oh the suspense is mounting. The crowd grows quiet."

"I don't believe this," the emissary snarled.

"I said 'the crowd grows quiet,'" Conal chided.

Lorkan flipped the coin once more and happily announced, "Tails. It's your turn."

"Ah well," Conal sighed with disappointment. "As usual, I never win anything." Turning back to the emissary, he knitted his brow at him. "What were you saying?"

"Do you know who I am?" the man snarled.

"Nope." Conal turned to Lorkan and hooked a thumb at the man. "Do you know him?"

Lorkan shrugged. "Never seen him before in my life."

"What are your names?" the emissary angrily commanded.

"You don't know who we are?" Conal asked as though surprised.

"Of course not."

"I guess that makes us even. Listen bub, tell her highness that if she wants to see General Firyn, she needs to come here."

"What?" the emissary exploded. "*General* Firyn? Who does he think he is? Where is he? I will not stand for this insubordination." He went to spur his horse forward when Conal grabbed the reins.

"I wouldn't do that if I were you… friend," Conal threatened.

The emissary's eyes blazed at him, but movement out the corners of his eyes caused him to look up to see a dozen or more soldiers with death in their eyes heading his way. Wheeling is horse around he galloped away, yelling back over his shoulder, "You'll pay for this."

"Well played, m'Lord," Lorkan chuckled.

"Well played yourself," Conal complimented. "Now let's see if we get any reaction."

It wasn't long before the emissary returned with a dozen soldiers who fanned out behind him.

"I demand to see Firyn."

Conal looked at him then the soldiers with him before snorting a laugh. "Really? You come here with twelve soldiers to compel the general to go with you? Are you that stupid? Like I said before, tell her highness that she needs to come here… and take your kids with you." He craned his neck to look up at the early evening sky. "Besides, it's almost dinner time. Tell her to come by after dinner."

"But…but, Firyn has to come, now. She commands him to come."

"She *commands* him?" Conal's face hardened. "Listen junior, you and I are stuck in the middle between two stubborn commanders. You do realize that this will go on all night until one of them sucks it up and goes to see the other. Tell you what. Let's see if we can get them to meet in the middle between the two armies, sort of neutral ground. That way both their vanities can be salved and maybe we can get on with taking the city. Do you agree?"

The emissary pondered a moment before nodding. "What you say makes sense. I'll be back."

Conal watched him ride away, the soldiers with him relieved that that they were not needed.

Lorkan stepped closer to him and lowered his voice. "Storri should be in position by now."

"Good. I want to wait until it's almost dark before we attack."

Ten minutes later, the emissary was back.

"What did she say?"

The man sighed in frustration. "No change. She wants him to come to her."

"I figured as much," Conal kindly said. "Tell you what. Why not stay for a bit, have something to eat with us and when she wants to know what took you so long, you can say that you were arguing for her. We've got excellent cooks."

The man grinned. "That's the best offer I've had today." He dismounted and stepped closer to Conal and Lorkan. "Name's Kieve, Captain Kieve of Commander Hafgan's staff."

"Welcome Captain. I'm Conal and this is Lorkan, commanders in this army." Turning to a soldier close by, he said, "Take Captain Kieve to the kitchen. Make sure he gets the royal treatment along with our best ale."

"Yes m'Lord."

Kieve stiffened. "M'Lord?"

"It's a sort of running joke," Lorkan hastened to say, giving the soldier an evil look and intoning, "Most people only say it behind his back." He looked back at Kieve. "I'll tell you the tale when we come back to join you."

"Ah," Kieve nodded in understanding, assuming it was some foolish act done in the ignorance of youth. Allowing himself to be led away, he was soon separated from his horse only to discover no one was cooking anything. All too quickly, he was tied and gagged.

"That was close," Conal muttered. Casting another glance at the darkening sky, he was about to announce, "Spread the word," when he saw two enormous shapes filling the sky, followed by an alarm in the enemy camp.

Yet the alarm was late for billows of fire suddenly erupted from the dragons' mouths as they descended and swept across the enemy's encampment.

CHAPTER 9

Gwen

"No!"

Aimil's horrified scream echoed off the wrecked buildings along the street. Gwen could only imagine what she must be feeling. With the *bunús* destroyed, Aimil would never again feel magic coursing through her. She slumped to the ground, tears streaming down her cheeks.

"What did you do?" Kalan asked.

"I took away her power," Gwen replied. "But she's still a threat. We need to keep her close. The last thing we need is her running off to report to Torian."

"What about the guards?"

Gwen looked around them and shrugged. "What about them?"

"Not these ones." Kalan waved a hand at the surrounding city. "Judging by the bell towers, I'm sure we'll be surrounded soon."

Gwen was torn between staying to spread their message of need and leaving the city to wait and see who showed up in support. Lyra shifted back into her elven form and forced Aimil to her feet.

"We should get moving away from here," Gwen decided. "Let's get closer to the noble district. There should be less chaos there."

They marched up the street together, Lyra pushing Aimil and keeping watch over her. Gwen glanced at her rival and saw she was listless, moving along only because Lyra forced her to. For a brief moment, she felt pity for the woman, but then she reminded herself of what Aimil had done in Auleavell and the pity quickly fled.

Gwen turned her attention ahead, where a battle was raging. Commoners were fighting against armed soldiers. The soldiers were outnumbered, but they held the advantage with better weapons and armor.

"We'll go around," Gwen said.

"We have to help them," Kalan argued. "They'll be slaughtered. And we both know we started this."

"Go," Lyra said. "I'll stay here with Aimil."

Gwen hesitated for a moment, then sprinted toward the battle. Kalan ran beside her, a boyish grin plastered on his face. An overturned merchant wagon was in the street, its fresh fruits spewed everywhere. As the press of bodies grew, they stomped on the goods, slicking the cobblestones. One person slipped and fell, and was promptly stabbed in the chest by a soldier.

Kalan went for him, tackling the man to the ground and using the power of his steel skin rune to crush the soldier's helm, along with his head. Blood sprayed through the slit in the helmet, splattering Kalan's face. Gwen's stomach churned at the sight, but she ignored her revulsion and grabbed ahold of a soldier, ripping his helmet off and casting him aside like a ragdoll with her might rune. He slammed into the wagon, his face cracking hard on one of the wheels. More soldiers joined the fray, but they were still outnumbered as Kalan tore through their ranks.

He picked up a sword from a dead soldier and became a whirlwind of death. He thrust and spun, blocked and dodged, his footwork a blur of movement. Gwen could see why Kalan wanted to be a warrior—he was born for it. Her attention was diverted as a soldier came around the wagon. He wielded a hefty ax and swung at her, narrowly missing as she backpedaled and summoned her fire rune. A wave of heat and flames struck the soldier and sent him reeling into the cart, which caught fire.

Gwen backed away as the inferno spread, and the battle momentarily lapsed as the heat forced everyone away. Kalan shielded his eyes with his free hand and drove one of the soldiers into the flames. His screams filled the air as his armor heated, melting flesh and hair, the stench fouler than anything Gwen had smelled before.

The remaining soldiers retreated, turning and fleeing into the noble district. The crowd of people shouted a cheer of victory and gave chase. Kalan rushed along with them, and Gwen looked back at Lyra, concerned about their group getting split apart. Lyra waved her on and motioned to the east.

I'll meet you outside the city. Do what must be done.

Her voice penetrated Gwen's mind, jarring and unexpected. Her words were like a headache, pounding with each syllable. Gwen nodded and followed the mob, pushing through until she was beside Kalan. He was covered in blood, gore, and sweat, and was barely recognizable. He added his voice to the cheering as one of the escaping soldiers fell and was trampled to death.

This is madness, Gwen thought. *So much blood and death.*

And yet, she knew it was a necessary evil. Torian would not give any respite, and she was determined to do the same. If her conscious was scarred, so be it. If she had nightmares for the rest of her life, but the people were free from tyranny, so be it. It would all be worth it in the end. It had to be.

The crowd continued to grow as the word spread throughout the city. Farmers came with their pitchforks and scythes, metalworkers wielded hammers, and others had collected weapons from fallen soldiers. The ragtag band of common people slashed and burned their way through the noble district, killing the soldiers and rounding up the nobles. Gwen convinced the people to take them as prisoners, finding some solace knowing that not everyone would be killed.

As the hours passed, more and more of the city fell under Gwen's authority. Soldiers began surrendering or fleeing the city entirely. The few who tried to fight were crushed immediately, their bodies drug through the streets as a warning sign to those who would side with Torian. By the time Gwen's army reached the duke's castle, the city was hers and the duke willingly opened his doors.

Gwen didn't spare him. The people wanted his head, and she gave it to them.

The mages from the Great Library have arrived, Lyra informed her. With the city won, she and Kalan cleaned themselves and washed their clothes in the duke's chambers, then organized the people into two groups, those who would stay in Wespin and those who would march on Havengarde. Gwen appointed leaders among the people and took a count of the men and women that would be marching with her. She was disappointed to find that their numbers were only two thousand but knew it was much better than where they had started.

Kalan chose a handful of people as personal guards for Gwen and they escorted her outside the city to meet with the mages. As Gwen approached, she spotted a mage that stood out from the others. He was tall, towering over everyone else by at least a foot. His head was bald and his arms were covered in runes. The man's most prominent feature was his hooded eyes. They captured her attention and sent a chill down her back. He wore flowing robes that were dyed a vibrant blue and he smiled broadly when he spotted her.

"Quinlee," he greeted, bowing low. "I am Menjing, Your Majesty. It is an honor to join your cause. My mages and I are at your service."

"The honor is mine," Gwen replied. "And please, call me Gwen."

Menjing's smile grew bigger. "The Librarian mentioned you might say that. Very well, Gwen. What is your wish?"

"My wish?" Gwen's brows knitted with her confusion.

"Yes. What do you want us to do?"

"Oh, right. We've secured the city and have an army of two thousand men and women who will march with us to Havengarde. You will help me with drawing the attention of Torian's mages. We will be a diversion and keep him focused on us until Conal and his forces can strike from the west."

"Very good. How will we serve as a diversion? Will we attack the walls to enter the city?"

"That would be the ideal situation," Gwen said. "Though I don't want to assume it will be as easy as it sounds."

"Many of my mages are offensive casters. We will overcome the walls of Havengarde like the waves overcome the ship."

Gwen found his description poetic, but she doubted Torian and his forces would be so easily defeated. "What kind of runes do they have?"

"Our runes range widely," Menjing replied. "We can call fire and lightning, run like the wind, and shatter stone like glass. Those are only a few of our talents."

"Are they battle-tested? It's one thing to say you can kill a man, and another to do it. Trust me, I know firsthand."

"There are a few who have seen battle, but most of their hands have not seen blood. But do not worry," Menjing added, seeing Gwen's frown. "They are capable and want to see Isentol change for the better."

Gwen was worried he might not know his mages as well as he thought, but they were the only spellcasters she had. "We will leave in the morning. You'll find lodging and food in the city, but try not to let them overindulge. A sour stomach and a headache will make the trip worse than it already is."

"As you command," Menjing said, bowing again.

As the darkness of night covered the city in shadows, Gwen met with her army's leaders one more time to go over the many details she had no experience with. Supply lines, materials for their camp, and a weapons shortage were talked about the most. By the time the details had been finalized and Gwen was able to get some rest, she fell asleep immediately.

Morning came and Gwen opened her bleary eyes to see Kalan standing over her. For a moment, she forgot where she was and sat up quickly. A glance around the room reminded her and she breathed slower, trying to calm her racing heart.

"What news?" she asked, yawning and rising out of bed. She had been so tired she'd slept with her boots on.

"Korla says Conal and his forces reached Gorwick."

"That's good, right?"

"Yes," Kalan replied, smiling. "Would you like me to fill you in after you're fully awake?"

Gwen scowled at him. "No. Tell me now."

"They've passed themselves off as one of Torian's companies and have made contact with someone named Hafgan, apparently one of Torian's commanders. Korla seemed distracted, so I didn't get much out of her besides that. And I kept seeing images of an old woman." Kalan shrugged.

"We need to get moving," Gwen said. "It'll take Conal at least two days to reach Havengarde, and we need to be there before him."

"I've already met with the others, and everything is in order. All we need is your word."

"You have it."

When Gwen had heard that their forces only numbered at two thousand, she knew that wasn't enough, but also that it didn't seem like much. As the procession began the march north, Gwen realized that two thousand people was more than she thought. The line of people stretched on and on, making her wonder how they would reach Havengarde with any element of surprise.

They marched all day, stopping just before dusk to set up camp and rest. The next day started slowly as most of the people were sluggish and exhausted. Gwen tried to be patient and had to remind herself several times that these people weren't disciplined soldiers. She wasn't a soldier either, but she also wasn't the same ignorant girl who had left Dawsbury.

After another day of travel, the walls of Havengarde were within view. The fortress jutted up from the ground, an unnatural structure amidst a wild, untamed landscape. Her motley army set up camp safely away from the place, out of range of arrows and, hopefully, magical attacks. Kalan forged ahead to scout the area near the castle and ensure there were no hidden surprises.

Night fell, and Gwen sat in her tent, unable to sleep. There was so much uncertainty, and Kalan couldn't get ahold of Korla, which made her worry that something was wrong. She absently traced the lightning rune on her hand as she stared at the wall of the tent, her mind roaming endlessly.

A sound outside broke her reverie and she looked up as a hooded figure stepped into her tent. She thought it was Menjing, but then she saw the body of one of her guards on the ground outside. Her heart skipped a beat and before she could summon the magic of one of her runes, the figure drew a sword.

"My master Grimmar sends his regards."

CHAPTER 10

Conal

"Get ready," Conal yelled, his voice rising above the tumult in front of the city. Raging fire consumed catapults and battering rams while soldiers staggered and fell, flames engulfing their bodies. A few archers launched feeble attempts to bring down a dragon, but mostly dodged the spewing flames.

Conal turned an excited eye to Bedo who stood next to him, a ram's horn in his hand. "Now, Bedo."

Bedo raised the horn to his lips and blew three loud blasts.

As Lorkan's army surged forward and Storri's dwarves emerged from the forest, Bedo stepped in front of Conal. "General Lorkan told me to remind you that you command, m'Lord."

The runes tingled on Conal and he paced like a caged animal, the urge to join the battle tormenting him, but he forced himself to take deep breaths and remember who he was. Yet one part of his brain argued how could his soldiers respect him if he wasn't in the middle of the fray while the other part argued that he was in charge and responsible for every soldier in his army.

His army… the thought startled him for up to now, they had been Lorkan's soldiers or Storri's dwarves. But combined, they were *his* army. Sure, once he gained control of the kingdom, he would have his own dedicated soldiers and Lorkan and Storri would return to their own kingdoms, but for now, he was in command.

A pulse of vanity flashed through him until he remembered he was responsible for the lives of thousands of soldiers, that thousands of soldiers looked to him to make wise decisions, especially when it came time for battle. The thought sobered him and the raging torment to fight lessened.

"I need to get to a vantage point," he muttered to no one in particular as he shifted a glance around to find a high point somewhere.

"Besides the city walls, m'Lord," Bedo said, "I don't see anything around."

Madlyn walked up, nodding thoughtfully at him. "Can't feel a thing."

"Which means?"

"No mages around."

"That's good," Conal replied, "isn't it?"

"If times was normal, I'd say 'yes.' But times ain't normal. If you was attackin' a city, wouldn't you use mages?"

"Yes, I would. Where's Korla?"

Madlyn rolled her eyes. "She's lookin' fer a secret entrance to the city."

"What? Why?" Conal redirected his attention to the battle, which was no longer much of a battle as the dragons had wiped out over half of Hafgan's army giving Conal's forces a lopsided victory.

Madlyn shrugged.

His mind already dismissing Korla, Conal urged his horse forward, his bodyguard moving in sync with him along with Madlyn, Bedo and Torgreth. They were met halfway by Lorkan comfortably seated on his horse, leading a defiant and chained Hafgan shuffling behind him.

"You have won another battle, m'Lord," Lorkan announced.

Giving her a brief glance, Conal smiled at him. "Status?"

"Don't have a final status yet, but the severest injury we have so far is a sprained ankle." He shook his head with admiration then held up the chain. "This is their commander, the dreaded Hafgan.

Conal stared down at her. She was a tall, muscular woman who was not unattractive. She wore the battle dress of a commander: padded leather pants, tall boots and a thick leather vest. "Why are you here attacking innocent people?"

When she didn't answer, Lorkan yanked her chain causing her to stumble. "Our commander, Lord Conal, asked you a question."

"Commander?" she sneered. "This young pup knows as much about battle as I do about cooking."

"Yet here you stand," Lorkan grinned, "brutally defeated I might add."

She said nothing, but her scowl remained.

"Why did Torian want you here?" Conal asked. "What was your mission." When she didn't answer, he leaned forward. "Do you who I am?"

"Of course not," she retorted.

"I am Conal," he slowly intoned, "King Kamron's son. You know who he was?"

Hafgan suspiciously eyed him. "Kamron in dead... so are his children."

"Wrong dearie," Madlyn answered for him. "Kamron had two children. But you know that. That's why you're here. You were supposed to draw him out and kill him." She suddenly turned to Conal. "That's why there're no mages here. Torian knew you'd have some with you and mages here would've alerted you."

"That was your mission?" Conal huffed in feigned disbelief. "To draw me out? To kill me? You? You and your puny army were never any match for my armies."

"Bravely spoken, sitting there high on your horse," she shot back.

"You think you're a match for me?" he taunted. "You really think you can defeat me?"

"I'd carve you like a cold chunk of ham," she sniffed.

Conal slid down from his horse. "Unchain her and give her a sword."

"M'Lord," Lorkan startled. "No."

"Do it," Conal barked.

Lorkan hesitated, yet saw the fire in Conal's eyes. Flipping the chain to one of the bodyguards, he said, "Unchain her. Find her a sword."

Hafgan rubbed her wrists, shaking her head at Conal as she smiled at his stupidity. Now, at least, she had the opportunity to fulfill her mission. Another bodyguard found a sword, tossing it to her before stepping back to form a circle.

Noting the circle of a one-on-one match, others of Lorkan's forces joined in watching, surprised though admiring Conal's bravery. Seeing the battle proven enemy commander, many thought his decision foolish.

Conal reached into his saddlebag and pulled out two sets of iron bars connected by a short length of metal chain.

"What are those," Bedo murmured to Madlyn.

"Don't know. Never seen 'em before."

Lorkan frowned at the strange contraptions. "Do you not want a sword, m'Lord?"

"No," Conal nonchalantly answered. "I'll use these."

Hafgan snorted a derisive laugh. "You will fight me with those? You make it too easy for me."

"We shall see," Conal smiled, silently praying his nunchuk runes didn't fail him. Moving to the center of the circle, he began spinning his nunchuks by his sides.

Gauging the spinning bars, Hafgan sniffed in scorn and took the first step to press the attack only to find the bars spinning at Conal's side were now crisscrossing in front of him like a windmill. Brought up short in her attack, she feinted left then attacked to his right.

With his left hand, Conal flicked a nunchuk at her head, causing her to over-react and lean backwards out of the way. In that instant, Conal attacked as blur of speed, leaping and spinning midair as the other nunchuk whirled in a wide powerful sweep and embedded with a crack on her ribcage, resulting in an audible grunt of pain.

Hafgan reeled backwards, her breathing suddenly exploding pain, and her strength compromised. She lifted her sword too late as the metal bar smashed into her head and the world turned black as she crumpled to the ground.

Conal stood over the prostrate body, staring at the indentation in the woman's skull. She was still alive though unresponsive, blood seeping from her nose and ear. "You really think you could defeat me?" he loudly challenged before pulling up the sleeve and revealing the tattoo on his shoulder. "I'm the Cobra of prophecy. I can't be defeated."

The revelation was electric, and word spread amongst the armies faster than any messenger could ever deliver – the Cobra of Prophecy was their commander.

"What do we do with her, m'Lord?" Lorkan asked, staring at the woman crumpled on the ground.

"We finish the job," Conal coldly answered. "She was sent her to find me and kill me. She was willing to destroy an entire city just to get to me." Dropping the nunchuks on the ground, he grabbed her head by her hair while reaching for the stiletto in his boot. In one quick motion, he sliced her across the throat, wiping his blade across the fabric of her pants to clean it.

He glanced up to see Lorkan's look, a mixture of stoic understanding and disappointment. "What would you have me do? I have nearly killed her with these." He picked up the nunchuks. "I crushed her skull. There is no survival. Oh sure, she might live for a couple of days, weeks, even. I have seen people injured like this, stone masons who failed to pay attention when a stone dislodged and hurtled down to destroy their lives. The lucky ones die immediately. The unlucky ones lingered, the pain worse than dying." He dipped his head to look at her. "I did her a favor."

"I know, m'Lord," Lorkan acknowledged and nodded. "It was necessary."

"What's truly sad is that under different circumstances, she could have been one of my commanders."

"Torian's poison must be cleansed away," Madlyn wisely stated. She pointed at the dead woman then narrowed her gaze at Lorkan. "She had a choice… just like you. You chose to fight. She chose to stay. Not everyone's tainted by Torian. Those who chose to yield to him are just as evil as he is."

Storri strode up, looking pleased and disappointed at the same time. "While I'll take a win any day, it wasn't much of an effort." He glanced down at Hafgan. "What happened to her?"

"That's Commander Hafgan," Lorkan said. "She decided to fight Conal."

Storri blinked as his gaze switched between Conal and Hafgan. He noticed the nunchuks in Conal's hands. "You use those?"

"Yes."

"I've seen those used once before. Very dangerous weapons when used by someone who knows what they're doing. You're just full of surprises."

Conal grinned and shrugged. "What's your status?"

"We're all fine," Storri chuckled. "Like I said, easiest battle I've ever been in. The dragons were a nice touch, especially since no one has seen a dragon for hundreds of years. Almost terrified us as much as the enemy. How'd you manage it?"

Conal thought about Drustan and Meinir, deciding they would reveal their dual status when they were ready. "Pure luck. I'll explain later. Let's go see how the city fared."

The city gates were still closed when they approached. In fact, the city was much too quiet. One would expect jubilation, especially anyone witnessing the crushing victory of the army that just rescued the city.

The peephole slide in the smaller door within the left gate door scraped open then closed and the small door pulled open and a plump man stepped out with an ingratiating smile as he pulled the door closed behind him.

"Thank you so much for rescuing this city," he said, as though repeating lines he had memorized for the occasion. "We were in such dire circumstances before your... before your... timely arrival. Yes, you came in the nick of time. Thank you." He started to turn away when Conal stopped him.

"Whoa there mister. Who are you?"

The man turned back, offering the same ingratiating smile. "I am the burgomaster of the city."

"Are you all OK?"

"Yes. Everything is fine."

"Do you have enough to feed your city?" Conal asked, wondering why the man seemed so anxious to get back inside.

"Yes," the burgomaster repeated. "Everything is fine."

Conal frowned at him then said, "We will need supplies."

The man's eyes widened. "Supplies?"

"Yes," Conal emphasized. "Supplies: flour, water, meats, things like that."

The burgomaster's ingratiating smile vanished as he wrung his hands and started talking to himself. "Supplies. They never said anything about supplies. That wasn't part of the plan. They said it would be easy. He'd show up and she would kill him. Then everything would be fine. Never said anything about supplies."

"This is madness," Storri blurted and stepped towards the door causing the burgomaster to yelp and rush in first, vainly attempting to close the door behind him before Conal kicked it with such force that it sent the man sprawling on the ground.

Conal stepped inside followed by the others. However, once inside, they abruptly stopped. For there in the open space between the city gates and the interior walls were several sets of gallows, a body dangling beneath each rope. One set of gallows contained what looked to be a family: father, mother, and three children all under the age of ten. Looking to his left, more gallows filled with limp bodies lined the street as it curved its way into the city.

"What happened here?" Conal demanded.

The burgomaster's eyes filled with tears. "They killed a tenth of the city then herded the rest east towards Havengarde, my own family among them. We could do nothing to stop them. They said that if anyone said anything about what happened here, they would all die."

"Why?"

"You are the son of Kamron?" The burgomaster gazed at him, his shoulders settling in resignation.

"Yes."

Exhaling a long-suffering sigh, he wiped a tear away. With bitterness in his voice, he clenched his jaw. "Then it no longer matters for my family is condemned. She was supposed to kill you. He promised that once you were dead, everyone would return."

"And you honestly believed that?" Lorkan scoffed. "Wake up man. Your family was doomed before they set foot out of this blighted city." He pointed at Conal. "This man is your only hope. He's more than a king's son." He reached up to touch the sleeve covering Conal's tattoo. "With your permission, m'Lord."

"None needed," Conal replied, pulling up the sleeve to display the snake's head that shimmered with a crimson sheen.

"He's the Cobra who will defeat Torian."

The reaction was what Lorkan had hoped, for the burgomaster dropped to his knees.

"By the gods," the man gushed. "It's true. Save my family, m'Lord."

"I'll do my best," Conal reassured him. Bending down to grasp him by the elbow, he lifted him to standing. "Now tell me what happened."

Twenty minutes later had heard enough. "So there's no army close by?"

"That's what I overheard, m'Lord. Firyn was supposed to join Hafgan here and wait for you. Once you were eliminated, they were to proceed west. At least that's what I could make out."

"And the families they moved out of Gorwick left several days ago?"

"Yes, m'Lord, headed for Havengarde. They should be closing in on the city by now."

Conal frowned at Lorkan and Storri. "Why would Torian want the distraction of civilians in Havengarde, civilians who don't even live there?"

"Dragons and hostages," Drustan said walking up, Meinir beside him. "By now, Torian is fully aware that dragons do exist and that they are on your side. I imagine he's betting that you won't use them when you attack Havengarde for fear of killing innocent women and children."

"Which would negate the advantage of having dragons," Lorkan observed.

"Exactly."

"Where have you two been?" Conal gazed knowingly at them.

"Scouting," Meinir answered. "By the way, there's an army to the south headed this way."

CHAPTER 11

Gwen

The figure exploded into motion.

He lifted the sword in an overhead chop, bringing the blade down toward Gwen. She rolled aside at the last second and scrambled to her feet, rushing to the other side of the tent. The assassin came after her, wildly swinging his blade, the sword smashing into everything around him.

Gwen turned to face him and summoned the magic of her speed runes. "*Luas,*" she spoke its name, then charged ahead, slamming into the assassin. They both went flying, crashing into the center poles of the tent. They splintered under the force and the canvas collapsed on top of them.

A cry of alarm echoed through the camp, followed by shouts and the sound of steel ringing upon steel. Gwen crawled under the material, trying to navigate her way to freedom. She heard the material rip, and then something heavy landed on her. It was the assassin. He pummeled her with his fists, striking her over and over. She stifled her groans of pain and blindly tried to grab onto him through the material. It was soft and she couldn't get a strong grip.

"*Láidreacht,*" she gasped, then pushed against him with everything she had.

The weight was gone. She clawed at the canvas and finally pulled it off, emerging to a sight of chaos. Over a dozen tents were burning. Robed figures, more of

Grimmar's lackeys, were cutting their way through her army, heading for Lyra. She'd transformed into her dragon form and roared as she stomped the ground in anger. Gwen spotted Kalan. He was gathering a group of people, stopping those who tried to flee and bringing them together.

The assassin who'd attacked her was back. She had no idea how far she'd flung him, but he approached calmly. Clearly, she hadn't injured him. He spun his sword around with skillful comfort and threw his hood back. He was much older than her, and atop his head where hair should have been, the skin was covered with runes.

"You made a grave mistake in coming here," he said.

Gwen didn't bother with a reply. She lifted her left hand and spoke the name of the lightning rune. A lance of blinding white energy left her palm, forking through the air. In the blink of an eye, the assassin twirled his blade and deflected the bolt into the sky. Gwen watched in amazement as the lightning flew high and disappeared.

"Is that the best you've got?" he mocked.

He stalked around her in a circle, continuously spinning his blade, alternating from hand to hand.

"Your master was too frightened to come himself?" Gwen said.

The man laughed. "Hardly! Dealing with someone as pathetic as you would be overkill, so why would Grimmar trouble himself?"

Gwen launched another lightning bolt at him as a distraction, then used her speed runes to close the distance between them. Her might rune invigorated her and she punched him hard in the chest. She felt his bones crack under the blow, but she didn't stop. As the assassin fell backward to the ground, Gwen followed through with a wave of fire. His robes were incinerated instantly, trails of smoke wafting up from his charred remains.

Gwen stood there heaving in deep breaths. She was getting better at cohesively using the runes, but it drained her strength considerably. A look around the camp revealed that more tents were burning now. Kalan's small group had doubled in size, and they were working to put out the fires. Lyra roared again, but the tone was different. It sounded pained. Gwen scanned the darkness and spotted the dragon.

She was surrounded.

A host of robed figures were encircled around her, but there were other people there, too. They were oddly clothed with glowing runes on their arms, and one of them jabbed a spear at Lyra. Gwen expected it to shatter as it struck her scales, but instead, the tip of the weapon pierced her chest. Gwen cursed and ran for her. Kalan called out to her, but she ignored him. As she neared Lyra, she saw a pile of dead bodies on the ground. One was holding a sword and she snatched it up, then drove it into the nearest mage. It was a woman. She crumbled to the ground with a bloody gurgle.

The others turned to face her and drew their swords. Gwen jerked the blade free of the dead mage and held it up before her, having no idea how to wield it. Blood dripped down the blade and onto her hands. She'd rushed to aid Lyra, but now she was second-guessing her decision. She was outnumbered, one mage against a dozen or more.

"There!"

Gwen looked over her shoulder to see Kalan. He pointed and his group of fighters swarmed toward the enemy. The mages turned their attention away from her and she rushed toward the people attacking Lyra. She targeted the one with the spear first, swinging her sword at him in an awkward motion.

The man brought his spear up to block her strike, and the sword collided with the thick wood, sending powerful vibrations into Gwen's arms. Somehow, the blade hadn't carved through the spear. Gwen's hands trembled violently and she dropped the sword. What was she doing? She wasn't a warrior. She grabbed onto the spear.

"*Tine!*" she shouted.

The spear caught fire. The man howled as the flames licked at his fingers, and he tossed the spear aside. Gwen grabbed him by the throat and looked him in the eyes.

"*Draein saoil.*"

The man's eyes bulged as his life was sucked away. Gwen drained him quickly and dropped his lifeless husk to the ground. The rune wanted more, *demanded* more. Gwen turned to meet the charge of another man. This one had no weapon, but he came at her anyway, his eyes filled with madness. She used her might rune to snap his neck, ignoring the yearning that the drain life rune pulsed through her.

The ground rumbled ominously beneath Gwen's feet. One of the mages had cast a spell similar to the one Aimil had in Wespin, and the ground heaved upward as it split open, swallowing several of Kalan's men. Gwen struck the mage with a lightning bolt. He was too focused on his own spell to defend himself, and his sizzling corpse sailed through the air before tumbling along the ground and skidding to a stop.

Gwen spun around, looking for the next enemy, but Kalan's men had subdued or killed those that remained. Lyra was on the ground, a pool of blood soaking the dirt around her. Gwen rushed over and knelt beside her head.

"Venia? Can you hear me?"

The dragon's eyes were half-open. Her chest rose and fell as she breathed, but the blood continued to seep from the wound caused by the spear.

"I'm fading," Venia said. "The dragon hunters have poisoned my blood. I feel it burning through me even now."

"Can you heal yourself?" Gwen felt anxiety rising within her. It had been a while since she'd experienced the feeling. Just as when Tobias had died, she felt helpless.

"I tried," Venia murmured.

"You can't die," Gwen said. "We need you. And we're so close. We're here at his gates." Gwen pleaded with her, but Venia's eyes started to lose focus and her wound stopped bleeding.

"No," Gwen whispered sadly, stroking her hand along the scales on Venia's face. The magic was tugging at her, but she tried to ignore it. She knew the dark rune wanted to steal more life, but she refused to answer its call. The magic grew more insistent, to the point that it was starting to give her a headache.

Gwen closed her eyes, intending to focus on the magic long enough to shut it out of her mind. And then she realized it wasn't the dark rune calling to her. It was the life rune she'd received from the elf in Auleavell. She remembered what the elf had done, restoring the vitality of a vine, and she opened her eyes. Perhaps she wasn't too late. She laid her hands on Venia's face.

"Saol."

Energy flowed forth from Gwen and into Venia. The dragon was like a dark well, and the energy vanished as it reached her. Gwen refused to give up, sending more and more energy into the darkness. She was already drained, and the river flowing out of her was exhausting what she had left.

Gwen could feel her eyes closing. She fought to keep them open, to stay alert, but the darkness was so inviting. She startled, one of her hands slipping off Venia. Several blinks seemed to help at first, and she replaced her hand on Venia's snout. There was no air coming in or out. Instead of feeling panicked, Gwen was... content. As her vision faded, the last thing she saw was a faint light beginning to glow at the bottom of the well.

When Gwen regained consciousness, it was dawn. She was lying on the ground under the open sky, a thin blanket draped over her. Sitting up, she saw Lyra was gone. A few guards were keeping watch, but the rest of the camp was silent. Nearby, Kalan lay sprawled out on his stomach, snoring loudly.

The events of the previous night were a blur in her mind, but she remembered enough to piece together the fact that Grimmar had sent assassins after her and Lyra. Gwen rolled her head around, stretching her neck. She'd slept on a rock, and now her neck was sore. She flung the blanket off and stood up, rubbing the sleep from her eyes.

"Kalan," she called out.

He continued snoring, so she walked over and kicked his foot. His eyes snapped open and his body tensed, but when he saw it was her, he relaxed and offered a tired smile.

"I wondered if you'd ever wake up," he said, rolling over onto his back. He lifted his hand and shielded his face against the morning glare.

"You stayed out here the whole time?" Gwen asked.

"Someone had to keep an eye on you."

"You were asleep."

"I literally just closed my eyes." Kalan stifled a yawn and got up, brushing his clothes off.

"You expect me to believe that? You were snoring like a hog."

"Fine, fine. Maybe my eyes were closed for a little while, but the camp was in good hands. Besides, we both needed the rest. The gods only know what Torian's going to throw at us today."

"What? You didn't like his welcome party?" Gwen rolled her eyes. "They almost killed Venia."

Kalan grew somber. "I know. She left a few hours ago. She said she was hungry enough to eat an entire field of cows."

"I'm just glad she's all right."

"That's thanks to you. You healed her."

Fragmented memories floated above the haze and Gwen nodded slowly. "I remember. Sort of."

"They tried to kill you, but they also tried to scare off our army. It didn't work."

"Nobody fled?"

"Well, I wouldn't say that. There were a handful of deserters."

"I can't fault them," Gwen said. "These people aren't ready for what they will see today."

A runner arrived and bowed low to Gwen, then looked at Kalan. "Sir, this just arrived." He handed over a folded parchment. Kalan opened it and read over the contents.

"Torian is demanding we hand you over," he said, looking up at her. "He'll grant a pardon for everyone who marched here if we do."

Gwen made a noise in her throat. "He's a fool if he thinks it will be that easy." Gwen stared at the castle, eyeing the walls and trying to determine the best plan of attack. "Wake the mages. Tell them to report to me as soon as they've had breakfast."

Kalan looked at the runner. "Do as she says."

"Yes, sir." The runner sprinted away.

"What's the plan?" Kalan asked.

"To bring hell to Torian's doorstep."

CHAPTER 12

Conal

To Conal's good fortune, the army approaching from the south was two regiments from Clagmoran's home guard, commanded by a thick-necked bulldog of a man named Awstyn who barged in to where Conal and the others stood outside the gates of the city, demanding, "Which one of you is Conal?"

"That would be *Lord* Conal," Lorkan not so politely corrected him.

"Oh… ah… huh, never said anything about that. My apologies, m'Lord," Awstyn said, glancing around to see which one was the Lord.

"Apology accepted," Conal replied with a tired smile.

Expecting to see an older man, Awstyn cocked an eyebrow in surprise. "Ah… Lord Kilmaryn sends his respects, wishing he could send more but the security of the kingdom is equally important."

"I am thankful Lord Kilmaryn was able to spare so many." He curved a hand at Storri and Lorkan. "General Lorkan and General Storri are my primary commanders along with Commander Sorcha. You will command your soldiers as the fourth division of this army. Coordinate as you see fit. We leave in the morning."

"Yes, m'Lord." He smiled with contented excitement.

"War council in twenty minutes. Be there."

"Yes, m'Lord… uh where?"

Conal glanced up at the too close city, the ghosts of the innocent dead seeming to hover at the open gates. Looking back over his shoulder at the charred remains of the battlefield, he smelled the acrid stench of burned bodies wood then turned back to Storri. "How about we meet at your tent."

"As you wish, m'Lord," Storri replied, pleased with the specific attention.

"I'll meet you there then," Conal said. "But first I need to talk to Drustan and Meinir. Madlyn and Korla, I also want you two to stay."

Recognizing the tone of dismissal, the commanders slipped away to coordinate boundaries and liaison officers. Conal turned a sharp eye to Korla.

"Don't ever go off on your own again. What you did was stupid. I told you to stay with Madlyn and that is where you will stay from now on. Understood?"

"I was only trying to help," she said, embarrassed to be chastised in front of the others, especially Madlyn.

"You can help by being where you're supposed to be. Had I needed mage support, no one knew where you were." Conal then turned his attention to the two druids. "I hope you know what you're doing," he fussed at them. "While I appreciated the attack on Hafgan's army, you put yourselves in danger. Was that smart?"

"It was expedient," Meinir answered. "Taking the battle to Hafgan on your own would have taken too much time. Yes, you would have won, but at what cost? You now have your army intact and ready to go."

"Suppose some errant arrow found you like it did Bryok?" he pointedly stated.

"We have greater protection as dragons than humans."

"Wait, what?" Korla startled, her embarrassment forgotten. "You're dragons?"

Madlyn shook her head with maternal patience. "Yes, dearie. They are shapeshifters. You're a mage. You should know about that."

"I do, I mean, I've read about them, but I've never seen one in real life." She stared at them with fascination.

"Let's save it for later," Conal gently scolded before turning back to the two druids. "While I'm not happy about you two in the battle, I can still use your talents, specifically in scouting ahead. You can range farther and faster than any of my scouts."

"We can do that," Drustan acknowledged with a nod.

Conal regarded them a moment longer. "Are there anymore coming?"

"They're on their way," Meinir answered. "Hopefully, they should be here in the next couple of days."

Nodding thoughtfully, Conal said, "Would you mind doing a sweep once more before you turn in for the night?"

"No problem," Drustan replied. "We'll wake you if we need to."

As the two druids drifted away into the night, Conal turned to the two mages, shifting a pointed finger at them. "I have a feeling that once we get into Isentol proper, you two will be very busy." He narrowed his gaze on Korla. "When was the last time you talked to your brother?"

"Just a little bit ago. Gwen has taken Wespin. She has about 2,000 followers with her, mostly civilians. They're on the move to Havengarde"

"2,000," Conal sputtered. "How is she going to attack Havengarde with 2,000?" He began pacing. "This is madness. She'll be destroyed. We've got to hurry."

"He says she has some more mages from the Library with her."

"I don't know what that means," Conal brooded. "We've got to move."

Madlyn placed a hand on his arm. "It means she has some very powerful magic with her to make up for the lack of a real army. In this instance, their magic will more than offset the weakness of her army."

Unconvinced, Conal shook his head. "That may be all well and good, but we've got to get to Havengarde before Torian can throw all his effort at her. We need to make some noise to draw off as much of his part attention and forces as possible."

He abruptly spun around and headed off to Storri's tent.

"Well that was rude," Korla huffed.

Madlyn glanced up at her with a look of pity. "Now's not the time to sugarcoat things, dearie. You got your underthings all twisted and can't figure out why he's not goo-goo eyes over you. All you have to worry about it yerself." She swept a hand at the vast array of campfires and activity. "He's responsible for all of this. He's a future king. You? Like you said, yer just a mage."

Conal burst into Storri's makeshift tent, a tarp raised up with a couple of poles. "We got to move. Gwen's attacking Havengarde with 2,000 civilians probably armed with pitchforks and brooms."

"What?" Storri exclaimed. "She crazy?"

"I know, but we're gonna have to get going, march through the night. You dwarves, while you can't match strides with a man, you can march farther without rest. You can go days on end. That's one of the many things I admire about dwarves. You're strong."

"That we are, m'Lord," Storri replied, flattered. "A word of advice?"

"Please."

"Let everyone rest for now. Give 'em a couple of hours sleep now and they're be stronger later. We forced marched to get here. A few hours rest now will save us time later."

Torn between rushing off or listening to the wisdom of a soldier, he opted for wisdom. Besides, he was tired himself. What good would it do to exhaust everyone. A few hours nap would rejuvenate them all.

"I defer to your wisdom, my friend. Cancel the planning meeting tonight. We can do it in the morning while we're traveling."

"Smart move," Storri grinned. "We can move out a couple of hours before dawn. That'll give us plenty of time."

"Spread the word," Conal agreed. Sending several of his bodyguards to deliver the message, he headed back to his own tent. As he strode back to his tent, soldiers seeing him pass by called out greetings and he felt their confidence in him. *Let's pray I don't let them down.*

Bedo had a small pup tent sent up for him with a bedroll unfurled inside.

"Get some sleep, Bedo," he yawned. "We'll be getting up early."

"Yes, m'Lord." Bedo waited for Conal to stretch out on the bedroll before wrapping a thick woolen blanket around his shoulders. Settling onto the ground in front of Conal's tent, he curled an arm under his head and closed his eyes.

Though tired, Conal's mind wouldn't settle and he tossed. He was sure that he had just fallen asleep when he felt a nudge and heard Bedo's voice.

"Time to rise, m'Lord."

Conal sat up and rubbed his eyes. Crawling out of the tent, he heard the rustle of activity as fires were doused, bedrolls tied up, tents dismantled. Yawning, he shivered in the morning briskness, silently wishing for something hot to drink.

Numbly standing there, watching Bedo tear down his tent, he felt someone behind him and turned to see Drustan and Meinir approaching.

"Anything?" Conal asked.

"It's quiet all the way to Cwnbriar," Drustan replied.

"How far is that?"

"About halfway to Havengarde," Meinir answered.

Conal frowned. "Seems too quiet. Shouldn't there be some sort of military presence between here and Havengarde?"

"You forget that you've destroyed two of Torian's armies," Drustan pointed out. "Unless he knows his backdoor is open, he'll assume everything is fine."

Conal's frown remained. "He has to have some sort of communications with his military in the west. How is he doing it?"

"That's something you need to ask your mages," Meinir replied. She shifted a look at Drustan. "Let's find a place to rest."

Drustan nodded then told Conal, "We'll catch up with you. I doubt we'll have a difficult time finding you."

"Be careful," Conal warned, suddenly feeling protective.

"We will," Drustan replied with a warm but tired smile.

Lorkan passed the two druids, giving them a nod of friendship, and came up to Conal. "With your permission, I'd like to send out scouts well in advance of our forces."

"Do what you think best, my friend," Conal said, finally waking up. "By the way, Drustan and Meinir say it's quiet all the way to Cwnbriar."

Lorkan's initial reaction was to ask how they knew. Choosing to keep his own counsel, he said, "That should help us move quicker. I've chosen several scouts who know the area and can walk into towns along the way without drawing suspicion."

"I like it," Conal nodded, immediately understanding. "I want to place the mages farther forward. It's been too easy so far and I don't like it. Something's not right." Conal shook his head in misgiving. "I have this feeling like we're being watched... from afar."

"I can place them with my forward elements, if you wish. That way they'll be far enough forward and still have protection."

Conal mused for a moment. "What's the chance of us gaining more bodies as we march through Isentol? There has to be more people like you, willing to take a stand."

"We'll see as we get closer to Havengarde, m'Lord."

Conal nodded. "I guess we will. Are we ready?"

"Yes, m'Lord."

"Let's move. We'll do a war council wherever you are. Once I track down the mages, I'll send to them to you."

Momentarily left alone, Conal glanced around in the darkness, hearing the muted commands and movements of bodies to places in the order of march. The fact that he was in charge sobered him, and he was mindful of all the wisdom his father... his real father, the one in Urve who had chosen to love him like a real son, had preached at him. In this moment, he wished he had his father by his side, for the man always seemed to have the right answer and he would know what to do and how to do it.

Conal chuckled remembering a dictum his father would often say: *When working toward a solution to a problem, it always helps if you know the answer.* His musings were interrupted when Madlyn walked up with a still half-asleep Korla in tow.

"It's too quiet, my young Lord," Madlyn said. "When I was in Blasingdon, I could feel Torian's presence. Not his exactly, but his wizard's work, if you know what I mean. It was like a thick foggy morning where the mist is so heavy it clings to you. I felt it here for a bit, but now it's gone. It's like his eye is turned elsewhere."

Conal immediately thought of Gwen and locked a gaze on Korla. "Have you heard from your brother?"

"Not since the last message I gave you."

"Be careful, young Lord," Madlyn interrupted, placing a hand on Conal's arm. "Mind messages can be intercepted, especially by them that knows it's happenin'. I'm not sayin' you don't need to know what's goin' on. I'm just sayin' it might be best to leave well enough alone. If he's occupied somewhere else, all the better for you."

"Sound wisdom, Madlyn," he nodded, suddenly worried that all the previous chats the twins had might have been compromised, which might mean that he was being lured into a false sense of confidence. "I want you two up with Lorkan's forces. He'll position you where I want. I need all the advanced warning we can get."

Madlyn smiled in understanding and turned to Korla. "Come along dearie. Let's see what mischief I can keep you out of."

"What are you talking about," Korla grumbled as they walked away.

Despite Conal's misgivings, the combined armies made excellent time, arriving at Cwnbriar in the late afternoon. All the stress of scout reports, overhead searches for messenger birds, and frequent checks with Madlyn revealed nothing out of the ordinary. The several towns they passed through, alarmed at the soldiers, were hesitant about providing either supplies or information.

Conal was angry at first until Storri pointed out, "They don't expect us to win. You can't blame them. They've been living under Torian's thumb for so long that they no longer have hope and they're not about to get their hopes up because some stranger shows up claiming he's going to defeat Torian. Nothing will change until Torian is truly gone."

"You are right," Conal acknowledged with a sigh, "as usual. We rest here. War council at your tent in an hour."

Before Storri I had a chance to reply, Korla came racing up.

"Torian knows were here!"

"What?" Conal exclaimed. "How?"

Korla leveled an 'I-knew-it-all-along' look at him. "Madlyn. She's been working for Torian since the beginning."

CHAPTER 13

Gwen

The mages from the Great Library stood in a line facing Havengarde.

Gwen glanced at them, then turned her attention to the stone walls that protected the castle. She shifted her stance impatiently as she waited for Kalan to contact his sister. Despite her initial aggravations with the man, he had quickly proven his worth and had become her trusted right hand.

She looked over her should. Lyra still hadn't returned. She'd told Kalan she was going to find food, but that had been a few hours ago. The dragon should have been back by now. Gwen was worried something had happened to her and offered a silent prayer on her behalf, hoping that she hadn't been caught by dragon hunters.

"Good news," Kalan said as he approached.

"I hope so," Gwen replied.

"Korla says Conal and half of his forces will be in position outside of a tunnel that leads into the city. They're waiting for us to draw attention to ourselves."

"You mean we haven't already?" Gwen smirked. "Where's the other half of his army?"

"They're heading for the west gate, led by someone named Lorkan."

Gwen vaguely remembered him from the meeting in Haddence. "Good. Torian will be hard-pressed to defend his castle."

"What's wrong?" Kalan asked.

"Nothing."

"You look uneasy. What is it?"

"Lyra still hasn't returned. I'm worried about her."

"She's a dragon," Kalan scoffed. "She can protect herself. You should be worried about us."

His words made Gwen realize she was thinking foolishly. He was right—Lyra was fine. Probably.

"I guess we'll have to attack without her. How many archers do we have?"

"Not enough," Kalan said. "Two dozen, maybe."

"Do you think they can hit anything from here?"

"No." Kalan didn't even hesitate with his answer.

"Then we need to get closer. How far can your shield stretch?"

"I've never tried covering more than two people," he answered. "But I like to push boundaries."

"Try to shield the archers. I'll have Menjing and the others get closer. If the archers can take down some of the soldiers on the wall, we're better off. Once we blast a hole in the wall, it's going to get bloody."

"I'll do my best." Kalan jogged off to collect the archers.

"Menjing!" Gwen shouted. The tall man looked at her as she strode over to him. "We need to get closer to the wall. Is that going to be a problem?"

"That is no problem," Menjing said. "How much closer do you want us?"

Gwen eyed the distance. "A hundred feet or so. That'll put us within the range of their archers, but ours can't reach them from here."

"Do not worry for us. We are ready."

Menjing told the woman next to him, who passed the word down the line. They began walking together, moving ahead as an organized unit. Gwen waited for Kalan and the others, then marched with them.

"You should be at the camp to direct your army," Kalan remarked.

"You shouldn't tell me what to do," Gwen replied. "Besides, I'm not a leader. The people we chose are better equipped than I am."

Kalan opened his mouth to argue, but Gwen gave him a hard stare and he kept quiet. As soon as the mages were within range, a volley of arrows came hurtling at them. One of the mages raised her arms and the arrows flashed brightly, the wooden shafts incinerated. The steel tips showered to the ground, their pattering reminding Gwen of a hailstorm.

The archers grouped behind the mages and Kalan motioned to them. They readied their arrows.

"Our turn," Kalan said. "Fire!"

The return volley was pitiful in comparison, and a third of the arrows didn't make it halfway to the wall.

Those that did struck an invisible barrier and simply fell from the sky.

Gwen looked at Kalan and shook her head.

"We can try again," he said.

"Let's alternate. Magic, then arrows." Gwen whistled.

Menjing and the others raised their hands toward the castle. There was a moment of silence, and then a chorus of runes was spoken. The ferocity of the magic made Gwen wince and back up a few steps. Lightning bolts, balls of flame and spikes, glowing orbs of energy, and many other magical bombardments lit up the sky.

Gwen held her breath as the barrage struck the wall. Except, none of the spells landed *against* the wall. Like the arrows, they hit the unseen barrier and fizzled out. Menjing glanced back at her, his uncertainty evident. Gwen nodded at him, and they fired off their spells a second time. Again, the magical attacks were thwarted by the barrier. Gwen rushed ahead to join Menjing.

"What is that thing?" she asked.

"Anti-magic," he answered. "It's the work of a sorcerer, maybe a wizard."

"Anti-magic stops arrows, too?"

"It would seem so. Should we retreat?"

"No. We need the focus on us until Conal is ready. Keep attacking, but not all at once. And reserve your strength. The real battle won't start until we're inside." Gwen turned to leave, then paused. "Can you tell if the person casting the anti-magic is on the wall?"

"Mila might be able to. She has a rune that gives her far-sight."

More arrows filled the sky. The mage who'd stopped the first volley raised her arms and incinerated them again. Menjing summoned the woman he'd mentioned and she hurried to the front of the line.

"Can you see the one who shields the castle?" Menjing asked her.

Mila looked toward the castle and spoke the name of a rune. Her eyes went completely black. A few seconds later, she blinked lazily and her eyes returned to normal.

"Yes. The magic flows from a Prestige near the middle. He's surrounded by soldiers and two mages."

"We need to get rid of him," Gwen said. "Let me talk with—"

A roar drowned out her words and she whirled around, looking to the sky. Lyra had returned, along with three other dragons. Two were blue and the third was jet black. They flew overhead and continued toward the castle. The blue dragons opened their mouths and blasts of lightning flew forth. Lyra breathed fire, and the black dragon spewed a sizzling wave of acid. A cheer rose from among Gwen's camp.

Magic arced over the walls, followed by a barrage of arrows. The projectiles bounced harmlessly off the dragons, but a few of the spells struck the blue dragons and they screeched in anger. Lyra bellowed loudly and the dragons turned away from the castle and landed at the camp.

Gwen looked at Menjing. "Continue assaulting the walls, but remember what I said. Reserve your strength." She ran back to the camp, leaving Kalan with the archers. Lyra was conversing with the other dragons as she approached.

"You're back," Gwen said, looking at the dragon's chest for signs of the wound. Lyra's scales were flawless. Gwen's eyes widened in surprise.

"I went to find food and found allies," Lyra said. She lifted a claw and ran it over her scales where she'd been wounded. "Your magic is powerful. There's no scarring at all."

"I wasn't even sure if it would work," Gwen admitted.

"You have done a great service to me, but also for my kind. I am still able to bear eggs, and once we have the city back, I will help restore our numbers."

Gwen wasn't sure what Lyra meant about having the city back. She was just glad to see the dragon was healed and hadn't been captured.

"Menjing says there's a sorcerer on the walls that's keeping us at bay. We need to make some noise so that Conal can enter the city unnoticed, but we need to find a way to get past that barrier."

Lyra looked toward the castle and hummed lowly. "The barrier cannot be removed unless the sorcerer breaks the spell or dies. I vote death."

"As do I," Gwen replied.

"We can drop a few people on the wall. The rest will be up to them."

"Won't the barrier keep you from getting close enough?"

"The barrier blocks magic, but not living things. As long as you humans don't mind free falling a short distance, you'll be fine."

Gwen smiled, knowing just the person to lead such a risky endeavor. "I'll get a team ready."

She returned to where Kalan was and told him the plan. His face lit up like a young child on Yuletide. "Please let me go," he begged.

"The job is yours," Gwen replied. "Pick a few people to go with you. Once you land, do whatever it takes to get rid of that sorcerer. If you can at least break the spell and make him retreat, that's better than our current predicament."

"I'll do that and more," Kalan said confidently. "Be ready for my signal."

"What's the signal?" Gwen asked.

"You'll know when you see it."

Gwen wasn't sure she liked that answer, but she decided to trust him. She just hoped he didn't let her down or die as Tobias had. Kalan pulled the archers back to the camp since they were useless and handpicked seven people to go with him. Lyra was confident that each dragon could hold two people while flying near the walls. The small team armed themselves and climbed onto the dragons, all but Kalan exuding a strange mix of excitement and fear. He was enjoying himself immensely.

The dragons leaped into the air, their powerful wings pushing them higher and higher. Gwen rejoined

Menjing and his group, deciding to add her magic to the diversion. As one mage finished throwing a spell at the wall, the one beside them would go next. It kept a continuous barrage hitting the barrier while also preventing the enemy from shooting any more arrows.

"Tintreach!" Gwen shouted, sending a bolt of lightning from her palm.

Shadows passed overhead as Lyra and the other dragons sped toward the walls, diving down sharply at the last moment. Gwen couldn't see much, but she did spot the small forms leaping from the backs of the dragons and landing, thankfully, atop the walls. The mages continued their assault, changing the aim of their attacks toward the lower portion of the wall in case Kalan was successful.

The minutes ticked by and Gwen tried not to worry. Kalan was a capable mage and an exceptional fighter from what she'd seen, but his stone skin rune didn't make him invincible.

"The sorcerer is gone!" Mila shouted.

"Dead?" Gwen asked, but Mila shrugged.

"He's no longer at the wall, but I can't say if he's dead. The barrier should be down now."

"All together!" Menjing rallied.

This time, Gwen summoned the lightning and the fire runes, back to back, adding her magic to the chaotic mix of the other mages. Every spell struck the wall. The camp behind them cheered again, and Gwen allowed herself to be optimistic. Now that Kalan and the others had dealt with the sorcerer, where were they? He was smart enough to stay out of the way of their magical attacks, but where would he go? The entire city was crawling with Torian's men. She gritted her teeth and pushed the growing doubt aside, throwing herself into the magic.

They needed to blow a hole in the wall to allow the army through. Despite the combined power of their runes, the walls merely blackened under the assault. They weren't making any progress.

One of the mages pointed and shouted something unintelligible. Gwen looked, seeing nothing at first. Then movement caught her eye. The portcullis over the gate was rising. Gwen's eyes widened. Kalan was opening the gates! Gwen sprinted back to the camp.

"To arms!" she shouted, not sure if that was the correct thing to say. "We march on the city!"

The army was small and untrained, but they drew their weapons and shouted war cries. They were ready, Gwen knew. Ready to deliver vengeance for all the years of tyranny at the hands of Torian and his evil followers.

Gwen grabbed a sword and was about to lead the charge when a sound from behind their camp stopped her in her tracks. Her heart felt like it dropped into her stomach. The ground began to tremble and another sound overtook the first.

"What is that?" someone yelled.

Another person turned and pointed.

"War horns!"

CHAPTER 14

Conal

"Madlyn?" Conal cocked an eyebrow in doubt. "I don't believe it. Where is she?"

"Gone," Korla flatly affirmed. "Last anyone saw her she was heading for Havengarde. I bet if you ask the scouts, they'll tell you the same thing."

"Are you sure? She didn't say anything?"

"Yes," Korla snipped. "She said it was time to get back to where she belonged and then started walking up the road to Havengarde, walking at a good pace I might add."

"You didn't try to stop her?" Storri asked.

"I… I couldn't."

"Why not?" he frowned.

"Because she's more powerful than I am, OK? Satisfied?" She crossed her arms and glared at him.

Storri's frown deepened and he turned to Conal, hooking a thumb at Korla. "What's her problem?"

Still processing Madlyn's departure, Conal shook his head. "This doesn't make sense. She destroyed Firyn's army. Why would she do that? Just to make me believe she was on our side?"

"It wouldn't surprise me," Storri ruefully observed. "Those poor fools. All those years of training, weeks and months spent away from family, only to be used as toys for someone's blind ambition." He turned a hard eye on Conal. "When the time comes, and I pray it comes soon, that Torian comes to you in chains and begs for mercy… remember his crimes. He gave no mercy and deserves none. The same applies to those who willingly chose to serve him. Just like a dead tree cannot grow again, they must be ripped out at the roots."

Conal shifted a glance at them. "This goes no further. I want no one else to know, except Lorkan."

"What?" Korla burst. "The woman's a traitor. She had you hoodwinked."

"He's right," Storri sharply said, pointing finger at her. "Now be quiet, woman. You know nothing of military matters. What good would it do to tell soldiers who are about to fight and possibly die that the mage they trusted was a traitor. Is that how you inspire people to follow you? And speaking of you, what makes you think they won't believe the same thing about you?"

Korla's eyes popped wide. "But I'm not a traitor."

"So you say," Storri coldly replied then swept a hand at the assembled armies of men and dwarves. "Tell that to them."

Korla swallowed and blinked in understanding.

"If anyone asks," Conal said, looking directly at Korla, "Madlyn's gone on a mission per my orders. No elaboration, just that's she gone because I have her doing something for me. You don't know what then change the subject. Understood?"

"Yes," she sighed in frustration.

"That's 'Yes, my Lord," Storri corrected.

Korla glanced away so she wouldn't have to look in his eyes as she said, "Yes, my Lord."

Storri stroked his beard as he mused aloud. "She knows our strength and our position."

"And about the dragons," Korla added.

"Them too. Our element of surprise is gone."

"Not entirely," Conal responded. "Anyone seen Drustan and Meinir yet?"

"Not yet," Korla answered.

Conal curled a hand at them. "C'mon. Let's go find Lorkan and the others."

After explaining Madlyn's disappearance, Lorkan and Storri increased perimeter security in addition to sending out patrols. Drustan and Meinir arrived while they were issuing orders. Conal explained their situation.

"Madlyn's gone and our presence here is compromised. Gwen's committed to battle in the east. We have to attack to take pressure off her. You two know the area. What's the best avenue of approach to Havengarde?"

"The fastest way is straight up the main road," Meinir replied.

"Not exactly what I had in mind," Conal said.

"If Torian knows you're here," Meinir continued, "what does it matter where you attack from?"

"It would be nice to have at least one surprise," Conal sighed.

"You do," Drustan said with a slight smile. "We brought some friends with us."

Out of the darkness, five figures emerged, three women and two men, all dressed in the garb of huntsmen.

"Lord Conal," Drustan said, beginning the introductions with the women. "This is Derryth, Tesni, Amsyr. These two are Elys and Gawyn." As each was introduced, they gave Conal a respectful bow.

Derryth was a striking svelte woman with crisp facial features and long black hair. Tesni was a buxom brunette a hand span shorter than Derryth. Amsyr was the same height as Tesni, with blond hair tinged with emerald highlights that seemed to shimmer in the night. Elys was tall and muscular with a thick neck and close-cropped hair. Though a head shorter than Elys, Gawyn's broad shoulders and brooding face gave him an imposing presence. Two things were unique to them all: their eyes, coal black with pupils like the occasional flicker of simmering coals, and the numerous runes imprinted on their skin.

"There are seven of us here," Drustan said. "Four more are standing by to employ where needed."

"One more thing that ought to be mentioned," Meinir said, glancing quickly around to see who was in earshot. Motioning Conal and the others to close in, she lowered her voice and said, "Derryth says there is a way into the city and then into the castle." She motioned Derryth to join the group.

"There is an entrance," Derryth repeated. "As far as I know, it hasn't been used for many decades. The last time I was there was before Kamron's grandfather was born."

"How old are you?" Korla blurted, earning her glares from the others. "Sorry."

"How do you know about this entrance?" Storri asked, suspicious.

"Derryth is Princess Derryth," Drustan answered for her. "Her parents ruled in Havengarde before the Hunting. She will rightfully rule again when the time comes."

"How long will it take to get to the entrance and then into the city?" Conal asked, his hopes rising.

"I will lead them," she regally replied. "It should not take long, provided your soldiers are strong. It is through the mountains."

"Sounds like dwarf territory," Storri grinned.

"It is," Derryth said, "for dwarves carved it for us an age ago. The hallways and caves are large so an entire army of dwarves can easily pass through. Though it has been a long time since I walked those hallways, I have never forgotten my home."

"That means splitting our forces," Lorkan warned.

"I know," Conal pensively nodded, "but it also means getting someone into the city and castle without them knowing." He peered intently at Derryth. "How far is it to Havengarde?"

"You can be there well before dawn if you left now."

"How long from here to Havengarde for those not going through the mountains?"

"Six hours."

Conal thought quickly. "We attack at dawn. Storri and his army will go with Princess Derryth through the mountains. Lorkan and the remaining combined forces will continue this avenue of approach." He shifted his attention to Drustan. "I'd like to split your group between the two."

"Agreed. Meinir and I will remain with Lorkan, along with Tesni and Elys. Amsyr and Gawyn will go with Storri."

"What about you, m'Lord?" Lorkan asked, already knowing the answer.

"I'm going with Storri."

Both Lorkan and Storri were about to argue when Drustan spoke. "An excellent idea. That will get the king's son inside the city before Torian realizes it. I have no doubts that there are enough in the city who are ready rebel."

"What about me?" Korla interrupted.

"You go with Lorkan," Conal said. "He'll need mage help as soon as Torian sees the army."

Though disappointed she wasn't going with Conal, she was also keenly aware that Torian's mages were far more powerful than she was. Even Madlyn was more powerful. Suddenly feeling inadequate, she meekly nodded and tried to blend in with the others.

"If we leave, now," Derryth said, "Storri and his army will have a few hours to rest before the battle."

Conal turned to Lorkan. "You know better what to do than whatever council I could offer. As soon as the sun's rays rim the mountains, attack." He stretched out a hand, grasping Lorkan's hand. "We'll meet up in the city. Hopefully we'll have the gates open by the time you get there. If not… improvise."

"Watch yourself, m'Lord," Lorkan replied with a firm handshake. "Once Torian discovers you're inside the city, he won't stop until he finds you."

"And your sister," Drustan added.

"Torian is just a man," Conal snarled. "He needs to worry that I don't find him first." Turning to Storri, he said, "Don't worry. I'll stay out of your way."

"We serve you, m'Lord," Storri nobly answered, hoping Conal would be true to his word.

"Then we better get going."

While Lorkan gave his soldiers an hour's rest, Derryth led Storri's dwarven army along the road to the northeast, a road that would eventually connect with a main road out of Havengarde that went due north to the human kingdom of Tul Cragbyrn. Amsyr and Gawyn lagged behind towards the end of the dwarven army, scanning the area and occasionally drifting off then reappearing.

Walking beside Derryth, Conal noted she moved with a fluid grace, even at the pace they marched.

"Why are you so intent on helping us?" He said it without thinking. "There are so few dragons left. It's dangerous."

She cast a sharp look at him. "Havengarde was my home long before humans took it over. Will you return it to use or will we have to fight you too?"

Started at the brusqueness, Conal replied, "Hadn't really thought about it. I've been a little busy of late and to tell the truth, I hadn't even thought about what happens after Torian's gone. But I do know threatening me isn't exactly endearing your cause to me. The way I see it, there are eleven of you left. Humans and others eliminated the rest. Seems to me that your threat of continuing the battle only ensures your complete elimination."

That caused her to stutter-step, but she quickly recovered. They walked in silence for a bit before she spoke, though it seemed an effort to be polite.

"You are right, of course. I was wrong to imply any such violence for it is true that we are at your mercy, hoping that you will do what is right and honorable and restore Havengarde to its rightful owners."

"So a kingdom within a kingdom," Conal observed. "And what else will you demand? How much of Isentol will you claim belongs to you?"

"Now see here," she snapped. "Isentol was ours long before you humans took it over."

"And who did you take it from?" Conal shot back. "Are you saying there was no one here when dragons decided, 'Hey, this looks like a good spot. Why don't we build a city here?'"

"So you admit Havengarde is a dragon city."

"I 'm not arguing that dragons had *dwarves* build Havengarde. I won't even ask if they were threatened or volunteered, though it does cause me to wonder what treasures dragons had that they hadn't taken from someone else and used as payment… *if* that's what happened."

Derryth's nostrils flared. "How dare you impugn – "

"Come down off your high horse, Princess," Conal interrupted, "or did you forget that I am a king's son and when I regain my throne, a king. My family has reigned in Havengarde for over a hundred years… a hundred years when no one believed dragons still existed. We can talk claims to the city and the kingdom all we want, but the truth is that I have more resources at my disposal than you do."

Derryth's mouth clenched and she stared straight ahead.

For the next hour, as the evening's light slipped away to darkness, neither spoke and Conal wondered if he hadn't stepped over the line, that perhaps Derryth was leading them into a trap. But then, logically, she'd still have to have his and Gwen's support to defeat Torian. It was when Derryth abruptly stopped that an idea he had germinating began to blossom. A halfmoon's light gave shape to the forest on both sides of the road.

"We're here," Derryth said, pointing into the forest on their right. "Follow me."

Conal continued to contemplate his idea, so much so that he blindly followed Derryth dodging trees, crossing small streams, and clambering over rock formations as the trail she blazed continued to climb. Another hour later she crested on a wide rock shelf covered in vines.

Hands on her hips she sighed and shook her head. "I can't count the number of times I came out here." She tugged at several vines and pried them apart, Conal and others pulling and prying to give them space to get an army through.

When enough space was created, Derryth plunged into the darkness followed by a flash that lit a torch on the wall.

"How'd you do that?" Conal said, impressed.

"I'm a half-druid, remember," she lightly replied, lifting the torch out of the wall holder and handing it to a nearby soldier. "Torches line the entire hallway. Light only enough to find our way."

Soon, enough torches provided dim light showing the ceiling of the hallway was a good fifty feet above them. Conal immediately wondered how long it took to carve this from the stone of the mountain.

"This tunnel will get us into the city," Derryth explained. "I will get us close to the entrance so that we may rest before the attack."

"Lead the way," Storri grinned. Standing inside the mountain and seeing the work of his ancestors filled him with a comfort only a dwarf would understand.

Conal caught up to Derryth. "I have an idea."

"Yes?"

"I will return Havengarde to you in return for your help."

"You already have my help."

"Not this time," he said. "What I mean is, how much of Isentol was yours?"

"About half of it," Derryth answered, her hopes beginning to rise.

"Which half?"

"Does it matter? Human towns now occupy all parts of the kingdom."

"True. However, my thought is this; to start off, you reclaim Havengarde. Obviously you don't have enough dragons to enforce your presence. However, over time, that will remedy. But, until then, you will need help, so we enlist anyone who wants to stay. However, it will dragon law that rules."

"OK?"

"As dragon numbers continue to increase, you expand over a specified area that has been demarcated as the dragon kingdom. In the meantime, since the seat of my kingdom is no longer in Havengarde, it will need to move elsewhere. Likewise, I am losing a good chunk of my kingdom. So… I need to make up for that loss."

"How?" She looked at him and cocked and eyebrow.

"Tir Manach."

"What about Tir Manach?"

"You will help me take Tir Manach."

"You're going to conquer another kingdom?" Her frown deepened.

"Tir Manach has been under Torian's spell for years. My other family was murdered and Tir Manach did nothing to prevent it or complain about it. The present king is still under Torian's thumb. This will be justifiable reward for betrayal."

Derryth tilted her head to the side as she led them past side corridors, through large, vaulted rooms, and up and down wide sets of stairs before slowly nodding. "I agree to your proposal. Though frankly the affairs of men are of little concern to dragons, as long as we are left alone."

"Good. We can hammer out the details later. For now, where does this come out?"

"It comes out on the southwest side of the city. The city is built against the mountains." She went on to describe the layout of the city. One street ran along the length of the city walls, stopping well before the citadel. There were seven main thoroughfares that fanned out from the citadel all the way to the walls. With the citadel as the focal point, descending concentric rings of streets connected the main thoroughfares.

"The castle is much like the city with wide hallways, doors, archways, stairways, and anything else you would imagine for a dragon to move comfortably in the castle. The castle sits higher above the city and there are many levels within the citadel, arranged in concentric circles with hallways connecting each circle, just like the city streets. The throne room is in the center, a grand affair with a raised dais where the dragon king used to hold court. It is the throne room your father and your grandfathers used. I do not know how Torian has it arranged, but it will be hard to catch him unawares because he will see you before you can get close."

Not for the last time, Conal wished his highwayman days had brought him here. It would have made things a lot easier now. "Wonder how Lorkan's doing."

"When we begin our attack, I will have Gawyn find out where Lorkan is."

"Thank you."

To Conal's surprise, Torgreth came running up. "Storri asks how much farther?"

"We are almost there," Derryth answered, leading up a flight of wide stairs that thirty humans could have walked up, side-by-side.

True to her words, she stopped on a broad platform before a set of grand double doors almost as high as the cavernous ceiling and not quite as wide as the set of stairs.

"The city lies on the other side of these doors. We can rest now."

A few moments later, Storri came up and gave the doors a doubtful look, especially at the door handles well above the reach of any dwarf or human. "Who's going to open the doors?"

"Don't worry," she soothed. "I'll make sure the doors open when needed."

Conal glanced around as the dwarves settled in groups and quietly chatted or stretched out where they were. "How do we know what time it is?"

Storri shot him a smug look. "A dwarf always knows what time it is, especially inside the mountains. We made good time. We got another hour and a half before we launch our attack. I've got a regiment ready to open the gates for Lorkan."

Amsyr and Gawyn came up and drew Derryth aside to chat quietly.

"Amsyr says that Lorkan's army arrives unnoticed."

"How does she know that?" Conal sputtered.

"There is more than one secret way into the city," Derryth cryptically replied. "The attention is all to the east where your sister and her mages have engaged the magic of Torian's magical forces."

"Let's pray his attention stays there," Conal muttered.

For the next hour and a half, Conal tried to relax, but his pent-up nerves wouldn't let him, and he was actually relieved when Storri said, "It's time."

Amsyr, Gawyn, and Derryth joined to stand before the doors.

"Give us room," Derryth commanded, "lots of room."

Conal, Storri and the dwarves scooted back off the platform to fill the stairs up to the edge. Conal saw the reddish glow of the runes on their forearms begin to shimmer, brighter and brighter until the forearm was a swath of color. And then the transformations occurred as the human forms bumped and bulged and twisted as three dragons expanded to their original forms.

Derryth was a large coal black dragon with cobalt blue eyes and wings the color of shimmering onyx. Amsyr evolved to just a little smaller than Derryth, an emerald green dragon with eyes the color of liquid gold. Stout Gawyn was the surprise for he was almost twice the size of the other two, all muscle and power, his scales the color of dazzling amethyst and eyes that blazed bright orange.

A hush of wonder rippled through those who watched the metamorphoses.

Derryth stood on her hind legs and reached for the door handle then turned to Conal and Storri. "Ready? Then let's do it."

With a yank, the doors silently swung wide.

CHAPTER 15

Gwen

"Turn around!" Gwen shouted. "We're being attacked from the rear!"

She rushed through the camp to the other end, hoping the approaching army didn't outnumber hers. How would they pose a distraction now? Gwen tightened her grip on the hilt of her sword and stared at the impending mass. Something wasn't right. The army was too uniform, too… perfect. A mounted rider broke away from the group and thundered ahead, coming straight toward Gwen's position.

She lifted her hand, prepared to blast the rider from his saddle with lightning. The rider drew closer and closer. Gwen held back her spell until she was sure she wouldn't miss. And then she saw it. The finely crafted armor and the unique helm. That was elvish armor!

Gwen lowered her hand and sprinted forward. The rider wheeled the horse around in a circle, coming to a stop as Gwen reached him.

"Kirith!" Gwen shouted, a smile spreading across her lips.

"I'm not too late, then?" Kirith asked as he slid off his mount. He removed his helm and tucked it under his arm.

"Just in time actually. We're about to march into Havengarde. Kalan managed to get the gates open."

"Excellent news." Kirith looked past her to the gathered men and women and raised a slender brow. "This is your army?"

"It's small," Gwen admitted. "But it was all we could muster."

"That's not a problem, I just don't think they are outfitted for an assault. I'll have my forces take the lead." He looked back at Gwen. "If that's all right with you?"

"That's fine with me. We need to hurry, though. Conal is about to enter through the western side of the city."

Kirith retrieved a horn from his saddle and put it to his lips, then blew three short notes. His army split down the middle, each side going around the camp, and they converged back as one force on the other end of the camp.

"Let us go and take Havengade back," Kirith said. He climbed back onto his horse and offered Gwen his hand. She grabbed onto him and he pulled as she jumped, landing in the saddle behind him. He snapped the reins and the horse sped toward the castle."

"Attack!" Gwen shouted as they rode through the camp. "Fall in line behind the elves!"

Kirith's army was mounted and therefore faster, and Gwen's forces ran along behind them. The two of them rode past the line of mages and took the lead in front of the elven army, continuing to the open gate. As they cross the threshold, Gwen spotted Kalan and two others. They were covered in blood and running toward the gate.

"There's too many!" Kalan shouted breathlessly.

Gwen pushed herself out of the saddle as Kirith slowed, landing awkwardly on her feet. She hurried over to Kalan.

"What about the gate? Are the others guarding the lowering mechanism?"

"No," Kalan heaved in a deep breath. "The others are dead, slaughtered after we lifted the portcullis. I used my key rune to lock the door behind us, so that should keep them busy trying to get inside to room, but not for long."

"Reinforcements have arrived," Gwen said, pointing behind her toward the mounted elves.

Kalan looked, and the fear that he had seemed to melt away. He turned around and Gwen saw a line of soldiers coming toward them, all holding long shields in front of them, forming a wall of steel.

"You couldn't take them out on your own?" Gwen asked, cracking a grin.

"If it was only them that I had to worry about, then I would have already dealt with them."

The sound of marching steps echoed off the buildings that lined the street, signaling more soldiers were coming. The street was wide enough for two dragons the size of Lyra to walk side by side, and Gwen realized that everything in the city was built bigger than necessary.

Kirith's mounted soldiers clopped onto the cobblestone street and begin lining up beside one another, stretching across the entire width of the thoroughfare. Gwen and Kalan moved out of the way, stepping into one of the buildings. It was a small shop, and the place was empty. Tools and other items were left strewn about, and Gwen guessed whoever had been there had left in a hurry to escape the attack.

More mounted riders filed in behind their fellows until the line was six rows deep, then they began moving further into the city. Gwen glanced out at the gates and saw there were plenty more elves, but they were dismounting and entering the city on foot.

"We need to get to the castle," Gwen said, turning to Kalan. "I'm sure Torian is holed up there, letting his soldiers do the dirty work."

"This place is crawling with them," Kalan replied. "I don't think we'll be able to reach the castle without having to fight our way there."

Gwen figured that would be the case, but she'd been hoping to have some luck otherwise. The sound of battle outside replaced the echo of marching hooves and feet. Cries of both agony and victory mingled with the clash of steel.

"The real fighting has begun," Kalan said grimly.

The elven soldiers on foot began passing by, rushing into the fray further down. Gwen watched as their numbers continued to pour down the street, surprised that Kirith had gathered so many men so quickly. She spotted Menjing among the crowd and stepped out of the building.

"Menjing! Over here!"

The mage glanced around and spotted her, then pushed his way across the street. His mages followed after him and they converged inside the building.

"We need to reach the castle, but Torian's men are everywhere. Can you help us clear the way?" Gwen asked.

"Yes, we can escort you there. What of the sorcerer from the wall?"

"He got away," Kalan said. "We killed his mage bodyguards, though."

"He's probably gone to the castle," Gwen said. "I'm sure Grimmar will be waiting there for us."

"Torian will likely have his best soldiers and Prestiges there," Kalan added. "We're going to have one hell of a time getting inside."

Gwen considered Kalan's words and wondered what kind of Prestige Grimmar was. If he was a wizard, they would certainly be outmatched despite their numbers. She looked around the room. Each person looked back at her expectantly, waiting for her orders. She didn't want this responsibility, but there was no one else to take the mantle. They had come too far to worry about death now.

"Does anyone know the layout of the city?" Gwen asked. Silence met her question. "Very well. We'll just have to figure out the best route as we go."

"If we follow the wall around to the castle, that should mitigate how many soldiers we encounter," Kalan said. "Now that the gate is open, there's no need for the soldiers to man the walls. They've probably all been withdrawn into the city."

"Anybody opposed to that?" Gwen asked. Again, there was only silence. "Let's go."

Gwen and Kalan took the lead, turning back toward the gate until they reached the wall, then they ran along the wall's perimeter. Gwen continuously glanced left, right, up—wanting no surprises and taking no chances. Overhead, the dragons circled over the city. Gwen wondered why there weren't down in the streets helping fight. There was certainly enough room for their bulk to land. Gwen looked over her shoulder. Menjing and his mages were keeping pace. The buildings to their left provided cover from the side streets, and Gwen didn't see any soldiers on the wall. It seemed Kalan's assumption had been correct.

The castle was still a fair distance away. Gwen slowed to a brisk walk and tried to catch her breath, then asked Kalan, "Has Conal entered the city yet?"

There was a pause, then Kalan nodded. "Yes. Korla says they're inside the city. Conal's also headed for the castle."

"Is Korla as strong as you with her runes?"

"No. She has potential, but she's too fearful."

"Then we'd better hurry. If they reach the castle before us, Grimmar will slaughter them all."

They returned to a jog, but Gwen didn't feel they were moving fast enough. Her impatience was itching under her skin.

"I'm going ahead," Gwen said. "I'll make sure we're not entering a trap."

Before Kalan could argue, Gwen used her speed runes and left him and the others behind in a rush of wind. Her surroundings blurred around her, but as long as she kept her gaze straight ahead, she was able to see where she was going. The closer to the castle she got, the more she felt something heavy weighing on her. She tried to ignore it, but whatever it was would not be disregarded. It assaulted her mind with images, dark scenes of murdered dragons and large glittering eggs that had been destroyed.

Her breaths were coming in short gasps and her head began to ache. The pain pounded against her entire skull, and she saw tiny flecks of light shooting across her vision. She shook her head to clear them, which was a mistake. Her balance was thrown off and she had the sudden feeling that she was going to vomit.

Restore us, a multitude of voices spoke within her mind. *Bring us back to glory.*

"Who are you?" Gwen gasped. She tried to slow down, but the magic was in full control. The voices in her mind were clouding her ability to cut the magic off.

We are the dead, dragons who were murdered by men in this very place. Restore us, princess. Restore us and make amends.

Murdered dragons? She didn't know what the voices were talking about. Their presence in her mind faded and she had control over her body again. She skidded to a halt. Ahead, the castle towered high into the sky. A group of soldiers guarded the entrance, and other groups were scattered around the courtyard.

She was trying to count their numbers when something caught her attention to her left. She looked just as it slammed into her, knocking her into the wall. Gwen's body exploded with pain and she collapsed to the ground. She looked up to see a tall figure dressed in black robes standing over her. The man smiled, but there was no joy in his expression, only gleeful madness.

A jagged scar ran down the left side of his face, from his forehead down over his eye, ending at his jawline. His hair was dark auburn and cut short. He had no facial hair, and his eyes were green and bloodshot. Gwen had never seen the man before, but she knew who he was.

Grimmar the Mage-breaker.

Grimmar held out his hand and the air rippled briefly before a massive battleax appeared. Gwen realized that she wasn't up against another mage. No, she had the unfortunate privilege of facing off against a wizard. She risked a glance back the way she'd come, but there was no sign of Kalan or others. She cursed herself a fool, knowing she shouldn't have gone ahead without them.

Gwen slowly pushed herself up and stood. Grimmar made no move to stop her, and she didn't find that comforting at all. Her sword was on the ground at her feet, but she didn't dare make a move for it.

"Pick it up," Grimmar said. His voice was deep and his accent was so thick it took her a moment to decipher what he'd said.

"Why? So you can cut my head off while I'm not looking?"

Grimmar laughed heartily, then shook his head. "I wouldn't do that, little mage. It wouldn't be fair. And contrary to what you may think about me, I am a fair man."

Gwen snorted. "Right. Is that why your namesake is mage-breaker? You are a Prestige who murders other Prestiges. There is no justifying that."

"Murder is the wrong word," Grimmar said, tilting his ax. He ran a finger over the blade, cutting the flesh. A few drops of blood slid across the blade and it began to glow with an eerie light. He grinned, a smile full of dark secrets and lies.

"I'm an executioner."

CHAPTER 16

Conal

In the hour before dawn, three dragons led the dwarven army through the doors into what appeared to be a vast empty room carved out of the mountain. Glow stones lining the center of the ceiling gave dim light to the enormous room. At the far end was another set of doors made of stone.

"Where are we?" Conal asked, expecting to be immediately in the streets and heading to the west gate.

"We are halfway between the west gate and the citadel," Derryth replied, purposely slowing her pace so the dwarves could keep up.

"What is this place?"

"It is a secret place, a refuge when Havengarde was still Dragon-home. We knew even then that man would not let us live in peace." Derryth stopped and glanced around the empty space. "I remember coming here when Havengarde was falling. There were seventy-five of us then. We escaped the way we came in. Now there are eleven." She turned a harsh stare on him. "I have compromised our future because I trust you."

"We've already talked about this, remember?" Conal shot back then relaxed. "Besides, I like living near the coast."

Derryth frowned and resumed leading the way. Pausing at the doors, she said, "These doors have not been opened in over one hundred and fifty years." Reaching up, she pressed a stone in the wall. "May this room never be used again." Twisting her head to look back at Storri, she said, "Go to the right when you exit here. This is the outer wall. Follow it all the way to the west gate."

The stone doors silently swung open and the morning air swept into the room. The dragons burst through, unfurled their wings and leaped into the air. The dwarf army spilled out behind them, flowing onto the wide streets and fanning out, some heading towards the gate, others ascending the stairs to take control of the ramparts.

Conal stood to the side, momentarily getting his bearings. The doors behind him were cleverly concealed as part of the city walls that blended into the steep sides of the mountain. Tall buildings across the street blocked any view of the city and he suddenly felt clueless as to where anything was. Deciding to get a better view, he followed those clambering up the stairs then suddenly realized the sky was brighter than it should be at this time in the morning. But the brightness seemed to pulse like someone shooting off fireworks

He also found it odd that it was far too quiet here. That lasted until he was halfway up the flight of stone steps when horns blared, and the clamor of gongs filled the air along with shouts of warning. Racing up the rest of the steps, he paused only a moment to see three dragons spewing fire onto the streets below.

Kicking in his speed rune, Conal raced along the ramparts leaving his dwarven compatriots far behind, bowling over unsuspecting guards whose attention diverted to the dwarves swarming in the streets below.

Halfway to the gatehouse, Conal saw a mage hurling down fist sized fireballs that exploded and spread on the dwarves below. Unaware of Conal's rapid approach, he lifted an arm to toss another fireball when pain exploded as Conal sliced through his arm at the shoulder, the limb flopping onto the stone paving. Blood spurted out as the mage wheeled around and fell to the street below, only to be trampled by the dwarves heading for the gate.

Pressing on another fifty paces, Conal suddenly stopped, confronted by a mage standing in the middle of the rampart, waiting for him. Without a word, the mage flicked a lightning bolt at him.

Conal easily dodged the bolt and closed the gap, raising his sword to strike. Yet the mage was equally fast and Conal swung into empty air, only to find the mage behind him. Spinning around, Conal jerked his head just in time as a fireball flew by him. At the same instant, he flung his sword at the mage whose shocked face morphed to impending doom as the sword's point penetrated through his ribs and pierced his heart.

Wasting no time, Conal yanked the sword free from the crumbled body and resumed his race to the west gate. Thankfully no more mages appeared, and, leaving a path of destruction, he reached the gatehouse well ahead of the dwarves below. Bounding down the stone steps attached to the walls, he hustled around to open the gate, surprised by the dozen soldiers standing watchful guard.

"Yield," he commanded, brandishing his sword. "The city is about to fall."

The sergeant of the guard, a well-built muscular man, pointed at him and smirked, waving his hands in pretend fright. "One against twelve. We're so scared."

His mocking jeer abruptly vanished when the streets behind Conal suddenly filled with charging dwarves.

"Yield," Conal encouraged. "You don't have to die."

"Death before dishonor," the sergeant cried out and leaped for Conal as the swarm dwarves crashed upon them.

In mere seconds, the sergeant and the other soldiers were cut to pieces, not one soldier yielding. Frowning at the willingness to die in the face of overwhelming odds, Conal wondered why such men would choose to do so. Did Torian command that much respect?

"We need help, m'Lord," a dwarf called out, snapping Conal out of his reverie.

The support bars holding the crossbeams were just high enough to prevent dwarves from pushing the crossbeams out. Conal strode through the mass and, using his strength rune, effortlessly lifted the two crossbeams out of the way.

The dwarves watched in shocked silence for each crossbeam required at least two men to lift.

"C'mon," Conal ordered, oblivious to their stares. "Let's get these doors open."

Pulling the doors open, Conal grabbed a torch from the wall sconce and waved it side to side, immediately pleased to see Lorkan's army surging forward, Lorkan in front.

"We saw the dragons," Lorkan exclaimed, running up, " and knew you had gotten in."

Storri appeared by Conal's side with a smile for Lorkan. "Good to see you, my friend."

"And you too, my friend," Lorkan answered with a grin. "Ready?"

"Ready and willing."

"Then let's deliver a kingdom."

"Where's Korla?" Conal asked.

"She's coming," Lorkan chuckled as Korla worked her way through the soldiers.

"Drustan and Meinir?" Conal asked.

"Haven't seen them, along with the others. Don't worry, they'll show up in time."

Korla arrived with Awstyn right behind her.

Directing his attention to Awstyn, Conal pointed to the east. "Awstyn will connect with Gwen's force. Storri's and Lorkan's armies will sweep this half of the city. I'm headed to the citadel with Korla."

"Me?" she squeaked.

"Yes," Conal said, "in case I need your magic."

"We're wasting time," Storri growled.

"Right," Conal nodded. "Let's move out."

Dawn's light rimmed the mountains. Expecting to see dragon's overhead, Conal frowned at the absence of the massive beasts, wondering where they disappeared to. Dismissing them from his thoughts, he headed to the closest main thoroughfare, Korla racing to keep up. Lorkan's and Storri's army moved in sync, fanning out and pushing up through three of the main roads to the citadel.

Conal felt like he was in a tunnel with no roof. Though the street was broad, the buildings that lined both sides rose four and five stories high. The original dragon doors had much smaller doors cut into them, adapting to the size of humans. He wondered why humans would want to live in a city better suited to dragons.

At first, resistance was light with Torian's soldiers retreating in the face of the larger enemy. But with the citadel in sight, resistance stiffened, and archers rained down arrows from upper story windows, causing the armies to slow down for house to house fighting.

Conal's armies pressed forward, the enemy choosing to fight and die than surrender. Conal's speed, endurance, and strength caused him to slice through the enemy, the gaps behind him filled with dwarves wielding broad axes, widening the swath of hacked bodies and the dying. Korla did her best to contribute, flinging small fireballs or lightning bolts. Though effective, her insecurity with her own powers caused her to second guess her abilities.

By the time they reached the wide piazza where the seven streets joined just before the steps to the citadel, the fighting intensified with more of Torian's soldiers pouring out of the multi-storied edifice to join their comrades. Yet the combined strength of Conal's armies overpowered the defenders and they slowly fell back in a retrograde defense, taking the battle inside the citadel

Once inside, Conal hacked his way through the melee, dragging Korla behind him, up flights of stairs and down hallways.

"You know where you're going?" Korla panted, running to keep up with Conal.

"No," he replied, his sword at the ready as he led her down another hallway that abruptly intersected with a series of adjoining hallways.

"O my God," Korla blurted as Madlyn stepped into the hallway.

"Hello dearie," she grinned. "'bout time you got here."

Conal swung his blade to meet her.

"No need for that," Madlyn said, shaking her head then flicking her hand to the right and sending a fireball the size of a large watermelon down the hall to her right.

Conal and Korla turned their heads in unison to watch the fireball explode upon a dozen of Torian's soldiers.

"Whose side are you on?" Conal demanded.

"Yours, of course." She frowned at him, the answer obvious.

"You expect us to believe that," Korla sneered, "when you ran off to your master here?"

Madlyn rolled her eyes. "First, I have no master." She flicked a fireball down the hallway to her left. Instead of exploding, it spread like a sheet across the hall, blocking the hallway. "Second, of course I've been working for Torian. How else ya think I could discover his plans?"

"You're telling me you're a double agent?" Conal cocked an eyebrow in doubt.

"Ain't it obvious?" she replied, frowning at them then shaking her head in exasperation. "Think. What happened in Blasingdon? Do ya really think Torian would allow that to happen?" She gave Conal a hard stare. "You were supposed to be dead long before now. Ain't dead, are ya?"

"Then why did you leave?" Korla challenged.

"Figured you'd get here," she replied, tapping a finger to her nose. "Also figured you'd get lost unless ya had someone to guide ya."

"You know where Torian is?" Conal's eyes blinked wide as he lowered the tip of his sword.

"Of course, dearie," she grinned and winked. "Follow me." She curled a hand at him.

"I don't trust you," Korla snapped. "You're too smooth, too slick. You have an answer for everything."

Madlyn leveled a gaze at her. "It's easy to have the answers when ya knows the questions."

"You see?" Korla complained, turning to Conal. "That's exactly what I'm talking about."

Madlyn narrowed her gaze at Conal. "Yer wastin' time, dearie. Ya want this kingdom or not?"

Conal's lips pursed for an indecisive moment. "Lead on."

Madlyn turned and headed down a wide hallway. "This way."

"You're going to trust her?" Korla blurted, catching up to them.

"Might as well," he cavalierly replied, though his suspicious eyes scanned the hallway.

Madlyn set a quick pace, flinging lightning darts of fireballs as they progressed. Conal noted that the numbers of enemy soldiers increased at each junction. At one intersection, well-lit with ornate sideboards against the walls, Conal battled five soldiers while Madlyn and Korla dispatched twenty more. The next intersection proved even more troubling as fifty soldiers poured into the gap. Yet, with Conal's rune-might and Madlyn's and Korla's mage strength, they managed to overwhelm the enemy.

But cuts on all three of them caused Conal to warn, "We can't take much more of this."

"Posh," Madlyn replied, casting a disdainful glance at the cut on her arm. "Mere scratches." She paused and focused her concentration on her cuts, which closed and healed. She grinned at Conal, about to offer healing, when her jaw slacked open. "Your cuts... they're gone."

"Yeah," he shrugged. "I'm a quick healer."

"Not *that* quick," Madlyn marveled. "Has it always been so?"

"Yes."

They looked in unison at Korla who was struggling to perform self-healing, her frustration evident.

"You're tryin' too hard, dearie. Relax. Let your energy flow into yourself."

Korla tried relaxing but to no avail. "I still can't do it," she whined.

Madlyn gave her a quick once-over. "Yer not that hurt. I'll teach ya how to do it when we finish here. C'mon."

Arriving at the next intersection, Conal was surprised that no one was there.

"We're almost there," Madlyn reassured him.

Focusing ahead, Conal saw that the hallway ended, and he picked up the pace.

"Slow down, dearie. We'll get there in time."

Conal slid a glance at the mage, puzzled at her casual demeanor.

They stopped at the edge of the hall, peering into the vast piazza where the seven hallways met. Except for the numerous sideboards, tapestries, wall sconces, display tables, statues and other artwork, it was empty. Madlyn pointed across the expanse to the set of towering doors tall enough for a dragon to pass through.

"He's in there."

Conal stepped into the piazza, expecting to see soldiers suddenly swarming out from the other hallways, but nothing happened. Looking over his shoulder at Madlyn, he smiled. Lowering his voice, he asked, "Who else is in there?"

Madlyn shrugged. "Don't know. Usual he has Grimmar with him. But there'd be other mages hangin' about here."

"Guess I'll find out." He turned and strode across the floor.

"Aren't you going to help?" Korla fussed at Madlyn.

"Can't do no more," she replied. "You and me need to protect out here."

"But suppose he has mages in there?" Korla argued.

"He might," she agreed then ticked her head at him. "But if he's the one of prophecy, it don't matter."

Korla's frantic stare followed Conal as he approached the smaller set of doors cut into the thick wood of the grand set of doors. Her voice a whisper, she muttered, "Suppose he's not the promised one."

"Then you and me better find a place to hide."

Conal stood before the doors and inhaled a deep breath. Reaching for the handle, he twisted it and pulled the door open and stepped inside the throne room, a vast cavern of impossible height and scintillating walls. At the far end and in the middle of an otherwise empty room, a throne perched on a platform with seven steps leading up to the single throne. A sturdy muscular man with a full dark beard sat on the throne, a drawn sword across his lap. He looked up when Conal entered.

The man's voice carried across the room as though he were standing right next to Conal.

"So you're the brat who's come to take my throne. I should have killed you when I had the chance."

CHAPTER 17

Gwen

Grimmar lifted the ax above his head and his body began to glow with the same light as his weapon. Heat and power radiated from him, so powerful that Gwen had to use her might rune just to stay on her feet. Even then, it was almost too much. When he spoke, the words rolled over her like a thunderclap.

Gwen covered her ears against the sound, tears streaking down her cheeks. He took a step toward her and the ground trembled with his power. The buildings shook around them, and Gwen knew that she would not survive against him. In a blur of movement, she dropped down and retrieved her blade, then tried to stab Grimmar in the stomach as she came back up.

There was a clang of metal as Grimmar's ax blocked her sword. He rotated his wrist, locking her blade between the ax head and the handle, then jerked back. Gwen's sword was ripped from her grasp and it went sailing away, clattering to the ground somewhere behind Grimmar. Before she could react, Grimmar backhanded her. She flew backward, striking the wall again with a crunch, then bounced off to the ground.

She didn't know for sure, but she thought some of her ribs were broken. Gwen whispered the word, *"Leighis."* The magic began healing her, but it was a slow process. Gwen lurched to her feet, pushing the pain into the back of her mind. She matched Grimmar's intense stare.

I'm going to die, she thought.

And then she rushed him, lifting her left hand. She got close enough to touch his chest before letting off a blast of lightning. Grimmar grunted as he was thrown backward from the concussive force. Thin trails of smoke rose from his robes, but otherwise, he seemed unfazed.

"You've got nerve, I'll give you that. Most of the mages I killed cowered and begged for their life."

"I don't beg," Gwen snapped.

"We'll see."

Grimmar stomped his right foot down. The cobblestones of the street heaved upward, forcing Gwen's balance off. She staggered and tried to keep from rolling her ankle, quickly diving aside. She tumbled a few times, then got back up. Grimmar was there in the blink of an eye, his glowing ax coming straight at her head.

Gwen used her speed rune and stepped out of the way just in time, the air from his swing brushing the side of her face. She dropped to one knee and used her other leg to spin herself around. Using the might rune, she drove her fist into the back of Grimmar's leg, just behind his knee. To her surprise, it worked. The blow forced his leg to bend and he fell forward onto the ground. She stood and leaped into the air, intending to land on him and use her drain life rune.

She crashed to the ground, the air knocked from her lungs. Grimmar was already gone. She rolled onto her back and saw him standing over her, the ax poised inches away from her neck.

"This has been fun, but I've got a rebellion to crush," he said. The madness in his eyes had intensified, and Gwen pondered for the briefest moment whether or not he was possessed by some foul spirit.

The ax rose and fell, and Gwen snapped her eyes shut, not wanting to see her death coming. Something heavy landed on her and there was a clang. Gwen opened her eyes to see Kalan's face right above hers, his excited grin plastered across his lips.

"If you wanted me on top of you, all you had to do is ask," he said with a chuckle.

And then he was pulled off of her as Grimmar grabbed him by the back of his shirt, flinging Kalan across the courtyard. Gwen didn't worry about him. His stone skin rune could take the beating. Gwen rolled out of Grimmar's range and got up, her ribcage burning with fire. Menjing and the others were there, too. They quickly encircled Grimmar, closing off any escape.

"You're outnumbered," Menjing said. "Give up or die."

Grimmar turned a slow circle, looking at each mage. And then he laughed.

"Fools! This battle is already won." Grimmar tossed his ax aside, but instead of falling to the ground, it spun end-over-end through the air and cut down three of the mages. Their forms crumpled; puddles of blood rapidly growing around them. The ax landed in one of the puddles and the glowing intensified.

Gwen stared in horror. With barely any effort, he'd slain three people. He was a monster, and he was unstoppable.

No one in unstoppable, Lyra's voice echoed in her mind. *Even dragons can be killed.*

And apparently, they could read minds without permission. Gwen looked at the ax as it began to shake, then it flew through the air of its own accord, striking down another two mages. Those who remained used their runes to erect barriers around themselves. Gwen wished she'd taken a rune like that, and as if in answer, Kalan appeared at her side and used his barrier rune to protect them both.

Grimmar held his hand out and the ax returned, then he gripped the hilt and it vanished.

"Enough games," he growled. Grimmar lifted his arms into the air and clenched his hands into fists. The ground rumbled and the sky began to darken with unnatural black clouds. A myriad of lightning bolts dropped from the heavens, striking everyone and everything within the circle of mages. Cries of anguish and surprise rang out as the blasts cracked and shattered some of the barriers, killing those within.

Dust and smoke blotted out everything. Gwen coughed and covered her face with her arm, peering vainly into the swirling chaos. A dark shape came toward her, swift and silent. Grimmar's face appeared in front of the barrier and Gwen screamed involuntarily, scrambling back. He cackled in response, every laugh laced with his insanity.

Kalan's shield was still intact, but Grimmar tapped it with his finger and it flickered and died. Kalan stepped in front of him, blocking Gwen. He started to summon his spiked ball of energy, but Grimmar grabbed him by the throat and lifted him off the ground. Kalan clawed at Grimmar's hand, his feet kicking wildly in the air as he was strangled.

Gwen used her might rune and quickly placed one hand on Grimmar's wrist, and the other on his elbow. She pulled back on his wrist and pushed his elbow in the opposite direction. The was an audible crack as Grimmar's bones broke. Gwen felt bile rising into her throat and swallowed, forcing it back down. Grimmar's grasp on Kalan's neck was released, and he staggered to the side, gasping.

Grimmar hadn't flinched. He pulled his broken arm close to his body and lifted his other arm toward Gwen. His palm glimmered briefly, and then a blast of cold air sent Gwen reeling. She shivered uncontrollably and her teeth chattered. She felt as if she'd suddenly been thrown into winter. Her lips barely moved for her to call on her fire rune, and the word came out as nothing more than a whisper.

Flames roared from her right hand, striking the ground around her feet. The heat warmed her and pushed the cold away, enabling her to direct the flames at Grimmar. He came at her anyway, the flames casting themselves aside from his presence. Gwen cut the magic off and hit him with another lightning bolt as he reached her, his hand going for her throat. The blast knocked him back a few steps, but he recovered quickly and came right back at her. Grimmar snatched her up by the neck as he had with Kalan.

She gasped as her vision exploded with lights. Grimmar squeezed hard, but Gwen managed to wheeze the name of her might rune. A wave of strength flooded her body, strengthening her enough to keep him from crushing her windpipe. She kicked at him vainly, the blows accomplishing nothing.

Behind Grimmar, the smoke had cleared to reveal the massacre. Many of the mages were dead, their bodies nothing more than smoldering lumps of charred flesh. Darkness was creeping around the edges of Gwen's vision, but she forced herself to look at the destruction, to burn the sight into her memory. The gruesomeness fueled her somehow, giving strength to the dark rune. Gwen clutched Grimmar's hand.

"*Draein saoil,*" she whispered.

Grimmar's eyes widened.

The madness was still there, but Gwen spotted something else. Fear. He tried to release her, but the dark rune would not be refused. It kept him rooted in place, siphoning the life and vitality from him. The energy filled Gwen, renewing her. The healing rune flared within her mind, and her ribs healed instantly. Grimmar's strength was fading and he dropped to his knees. Gwen pulled his hand away from her throat, but she didn't let him go. She would not show him mercy as she had with Aimil.

Grimmar tried to speak, but all the came out of his mouth was garbled noise. Blood flecked his lips as he gagged, and more trailed from his nostrils. His eyes shrank into his head and his skin became loose. He aged rapidly before her eyes, but she didn't feel revulsion this time.

She felt pleasure.

"You will never again cause torment," she hissed, watching as the look in his eyes became pleading. Gwen clenched her jaw and forced the rest of the energy from his body. The life in his eyes faded, and only then did she let go of him.

She stood over his lifeless form for a long while in silence. She expected to feel guilt or shame for taking his life with the dark rune. Instead, she felt nothing at all. Her emotions were completely absent, her heart hollow and empty. There was movement beside her, and she slowly became aware of Kalan's voice. She looked at him blankly.

"We're not finished yet," he said.

Gwen looked past him and saw a group of robed figures coming toward them, and they didn't look like allies. She nodded at Kalan and pushed past him. She took a few steps and stopped, waiting calmly.

"What are you doing?" Kalan asked. "Get inside my shield!"

She ignored him. Torian's followers would never stop. Whether they were under the influence of magic of some distorted sense of loyalty, she didn't know, nor did she care. All she knew was that death was never satisfied. And neither was the dark rune. It was pulsing across every inch of her body, begging to release the energy it had consumed. Gwen didn't think, she just reacted, letting the rune guide her.

The nearest mage was torn to pieces by a swarm of shadows. Another was sucked into a dark hole that had no end. Gwen tore through their ranks methodically and sadistically. She forced a man to pick up a sword and impale himself. Somewhere in the back of her mind, she knew she was no longer in control of anything. The dark rune dictated her moves, her thoughts. She touched a woman and gave her a disease that ate her alive as Gwen watched.

If she was to become a monster, then this was how she wanted it. A tool of justice, dealing out death to those who deserved it. The remaining mage fell to the last of the dark rune's energy, her skin flayed from her body while she was alive. As the power of the rune faded, Gwen slowly started to feel like herself again.

She surveyed the carnage wordlessly. Had she really killed Grimmar and his mages by herself? She turned around and saw Kalan. He was staring at her as if she were a creature he'd never seen before.

"Where's Conal?" she asked, looking to the castle. "Is he inside the castle?"

Kalan didn't answer. He just continued to stare at her. Gwen walked toward him. She thought he was going to run away from her, but he stayed where he was. She reached him and wrapped her arms around him, then broke into tears.

Kalan hesitantly hugged her back.

CHAPTER 18

Conal

Sword in hand, Torian slowly rose from the throne. "That you made it this far speaks persistence." He snorted a derisive laugh. "Though do you really think your presence here is because you're some great warrior?"

"Does it matter?" Conal shot back, taking measure of the man. "I'm here."

Torian descended the stairs in slow casual steps. Expecting to see him in royal garb, Conal frowned in surprise to see him dressed for combat, but then figured it was logical since Havengarde was under attack. And then he remembered this man was his father's brother. Was there a resemblance?

"You're here because I wanted to see you for myself." Torian's voice was firm and strong. "Come closer and let me see you."

Conal strode half the distance to Torian, studying him as he approached. The dark beard and hair were flecked with grey. He wore a thin circlet of gold with an emerald in the shape of an eagle in the center. For all Torian's bravura, Conal noticed the occasional shimmer of chainmail beneath the sleeveless tunic of thick leather. Conal smirked to himself. The man was taking no chances. Still, the muscular arms said he had not been idle these past twenty plus years.

"Well, *Uncle*," Conal said. "Here I am." It was then he noticed that Torian's arms were covered in runes.

"Come closer."

"Why don't you come here?"

"As you wish."

Torian touched his speed rune and in an instant was upon Conal who stepped aside just as Torian's down stroke swung at him. On instinct, Conal raised the sword above his head and felt the heavy clang of Torian's second stroke. He bent down and swirled, his sword outstretched hoping to catch Torian's legs, but all he felt was empty air. Instinct had him leap and roll as Torian's sword banged against the floor.

Torian came at him with a flurry of thrusts and jabs, forcing him backwards. Yet with each parry, Conal noticed the force of Torian's strikes seemed to lessen.

Abruptly, Torian stopped his attack and gave Conal a haughty stare. "You fight well. I'm impressed." In a surprise move, he turned his back on Conal and walked back towards the center of the room then turned to face him.

He shook his head at his nephew and sneered, "You don't have the heart to command. I gave you opportunity to attack me from behind and you simply let me walk away."

"Only cowards attack from behind," Conal retorted.

"Cowardice has nothing to do with it. It's called 'opportunity.' You take advantage whenever it appears. That's what kings do."

"No, that's what *you* do. A true king doesn't have to rule by fear and intimidation. A true king is loved by his subjects. No one loves you."

Torian's arrogant smile vanished. "Bold words from a whelp with no experience."

"Experience has nothing to do with it. Truth is truth. It's a fool who won't accept truth,"

Torian's nostrils flared and he composed himself. "Did you come here to bore me to death?"

"No," Conal firmly replied. "I came here for restitution. Death is merely the end state."

"Then you have greatly erred, for it is you who will die."

"I guess we'll see, won't we?"

"You've forgotten one very important point," Torian mocked.

"Oh?"

Pointing to his crown, he said, "You see the stone of the eagle. I'm sure you've been told the prophecy."

"I have."

"The eagle will bear the vipers in its claws. You know that I am the eagle. You and your pathetic sister are vipers, though that is stretching the imagination a bit. But, the result is that you two lose."

Conal sniffed in derision. "You've conveniently left out the most important part. From the west a cobra will rise and strike down the eagle." Conal jerked up his sleeve, revealing the Cobra brand on his shoulder, the brand now a dazzling tattoo of shimmering greens and gold.

Torian stiffened, exclaiming, "Impossible."

Energized, Conal closed the gap between them, attacking a surprised Torian who found himself pressed backwards before parrying and delivering counter blows.

The two opponents traded strikes and jabs, circling around the throne room floor as the battle progressed.

"I'm surprised you haven't called in reinforcements," Conal taunted as they exchanged blows. "Or would that be admitting your weakness?"

"Weakness," Torian roared, arcing down a powerful hit that Conal easily blocked. "I should have killed you when I had the chance."

"You said that before," Conal mocked. "But then I suppose that's what you're good at, killing babies and women."

With an angry growl, Torian increased his attack, his frustration growing that Conal simply blocked or deflected each strike yet didn't attack himself, as though he was toying with him. At the same time, he felt his strength giving way and silently cursed Grimmar for convincing him he didn't need the strength rune, that he was strong enough and besides, he had others to do his bidding.

But what about all the other runes he had marked on his body? An image flashed of the excruciating pain he endured accepting the speed rune. Truth was, he had nearly died. Only Grimmar's ministrations saved him.

But these other runes? Grimmar convinced him he didn't need fighting runes, that he was powerful enough as he was. What he needed was mystical and magic runes, runes about insight and knowledge. None of the magic runes had worked. In that instant, facing his nemesis, the epiphany burst, and he realized that all the runes he had on his body were nothing more than sugar pills meant to placate him. He had seen what happened to others who demanded rune marks only to horribly suffer and die, for they were not mage-marked.

But surely he was mage-marked. He had to be. He was the king.

Doubt creeped in and Torian knew he needed time to regroup, to come up with a plan to destroy his brother's kids. Where was Grimmar? He was supposed to be here. What was taking him so long?

Sensing indecision, Conal pressed a furious attack, his strength rune dominating the weakening Torian. Suddenly, Torian delivered a series strikes that momentarily caught Conal on the defense. He was about to step back when Torian spun around and fled towards the rear of the room behind the throne podium.

Surprised at the retreat, Conal reached into his pocket and retrieved a throwing star. He had never used one before, but now seemed like a good time. Praying that the rune-mark worked, he flung it at Torian just as he opened a secret door in the wall. Torian let out a startled grunt of pain as the star tore into his thigh, causing him to stumble and drop to his knees.

By the time Conal had raced across the room, Torian had managed to stand and stagger thought the opening. Conal stuck a foot in the doorway to prevent its closing. Yanking it open, he stepped onto a broad landing with five sets of spiral stairs, three ascending and two descending. Torian was nowhere in sight.

Thankful for the embedded glow stones, Conal rapidly scanned the landing, thinking that, with Torian wounded, it would be easier to descend than climb. Glancing down at the floor, he hoped for a telltale sign of blood, but there was none. It wasn't until he checked the second descending staircase that he saw the throwing star on the ground and the bloodied handprint on the railing.

Descending the stairs brought him to long hallway lit with glow stones. Torian was halfway down, hand on the wall for support, dragging his left leg. Blood continued seeping from the deep gash in the back of his thigh. Conal was on him in an instant, bypassing him then spinning around to confront him.

"We haven't finished."

Torian looked up at him, a mixture of anger and fear in his eyes. Inhaling a deep breath, he leveled a paternal stare at Conal. "You just don't understand. Your father was tearing apart everything our family had spent hundreds of years building. You think I wanted his death. He just wouldn't listen. I had to do something."

"Murder my entire family?" Conal retorted.

"That wasn't my fault. Some individuals I called friends thought they were doing me a favor. I found out too late. Surely you believe me."

Doubt slipped into Conal's determination as Torian's voice had a calming effect.

"What about my family in Urve?"

"I knew nothing about that," Torian said, his voice soothing and melodious. "As soon as I found out, I had the perpetrators executed."

"Really?" Conal lowered his sword.

"Yes. I know you believe me. Now come. Help me get to a physician."

Conal took a step forward when a voice rang out.

"Liar."

Torian turned as Conal looked past his shoulder to see Madlyn storming up the hallway, Korla on her heels.

"Liar," Madlyn again exclaimed. She stared at Conal. "Can't you see he's using his voice to sway you?" She snapped her head to glare at Torian. "You're just like Havyrd Smooth-tongue – all mouth and no brains."

"Shut up, woman," Torian seethed. "Why are you here? You're supposed to be helping Grimmar."

"Grimmar doesn't need my help," she replied then pointed a finger at Conal. "Besides, he needs to hear the truth from you, the man who killed his family."

Torian flipped his sword up to stab her only to have it deflected by Conal's blade. Torian twisted his head to look at him, pitiful eyes pleading for understanding. "I'm your uncle, your own flesh and blood."

Conal felt a surge of guilt and stepped back.

"Stop it," Madlyn scolded. "He's using an emotions voice-rune."

"Don't listen to her," Torian continued, his leg throbbing. "She's a traitor. You can't trust her. Listen to me. You need to help me. You shouldn't have hurt me like you did."

"I'm… I'm sorry." Frowning, Conal gazed down at his sword as though he couldn't understand how it came to be in his hands. His first inclination was to toss it on the floor, but that didn't seem right.

"Does it hurt?" Madlyn interrupted, smacking Torian's wound.

"The gods damn you woman," Torian roared, cringing in pain as he awkwardly stepped away.

In that instant, Torian's voice spell broke and Conal woke to his surroundings.

At the same time, Korla stepped around Madlyn and placed a hand on Torian's shoulder. "Here. Let me help. *Glórach an Bás.*"

Expecting the pain to subside and the wound to heal, Torian waited but a few moments before excoriating her. "That didn't do anything, you stupid woman."

"Ah well," Korla shrugged. "Sometimes it works and sometimes it doesn't."

Torian felt he point of Conal's sword at his side. Turning his head to face him, he used his most persuasive voice. "These two are thorns in our sides. You need to get me to a physician. Then we need to talk about co-ruling. You'd like that, wouldn't you?"

Conal barked a laugh. "Co-ruling? Are you serious? You're not ruling anything anymore."

Torian's eyes blinked wide and he refocused his voice. "But you *want* to rule with me. I'm your uncle. You'd never want to harm me."

"What gave you that idea?" Conal challenged. "I've come to end this, remember?"

Madlyn shifted a glance at Korla, dipping her head in respect.

"You two need to step away," Conal told the two mages before turning his full attention on Torian. "Like I said, it's time to end this."

Dumbfounded, Torian stared at them before tossing his sword on the floor. Glaring defiantly at Conal, he said, "I won't fight you. You'll have to kill an unarmed man."

"Just like you killed my unarmed family in Urve," Conal retorted, swinging his blade.

Torian dodged the attack, grabbing his sword in the process, before limping back several steps then turning to force his legs to carry him down the hallway.

Conal let him go until Torian was almost at the far door at the end. Withdrawing another throwing star, he whipped it down the hall with such intensity that it completely sliced through the chainmail and imbedded itself in Torian's back, propelling him forward to crash onto the floor.

"Stay here," Conal ordered the two mages. An instant later, he stood over the prostrate body of his uncle who was struggling to push himself to his knees. Conal patiently waited until Torian sat on his haunches, blood gushing out the wound in his back.

"Any last words?" Conal coldly asked.

"Go to hell," he snarled, spitting blood.

"Not very original," Conal taunted, "but they'll do. Remember this?" He pulled back the sleeve to show the Cobra brand. "It will be the last thing you remember." In a powerful stroke, he sliced though Torian's neck.

Torian's head momentarily wavered before rolling forward and down to the floor. His body sat back then slowly flopped to the side.

Though watching Conal stare down at his uncle, Madlyn spoke to Korla. "That was very clever of you, dearie."

"Thank you," Korla smiled. "It was all I could think of at the moment."

"Where'd you learn the spell to counter a voice rune?"

"It was one of the things I was taught. Never thought I'd ever use it."

Madlyn turned to her and placed a gentle hand on her arm. "You're gonna to be a great mage, dearie."

Korla studied the older mage. "Were you really working for us all along?"

"How else ya think he and all the others knew what was going on here?" She turned back to gaze at Conal. "He's gonna need our help. He'll have to undo all of Torian's wickedness. That'll take time. And of course, there's the dragons to consider."

CHAPTER 19

Gwen

"Torian is dead. Korla saw Conal strike the killing blow."

Gwen pulled back from Kalan and wiped her tears. "Then it *is* over," she said. "We did it. We've taken back the throne."

"There are still many things to do, but the worst has passed," Kalan replied.

"Come on, let's go find Conal."

They walked across the piazza where seven streets conjoined and headed up the stairs into the castle. Bodies littered the area, and Gwen was forced to tread carefully to keep from slipping in the blood that soaked the cobblestones.

The inside of the castle was just as bad, if not worse. The bodies of both groups littered the halls. Gwen navigated through the carnage and reached the throne room as Conal and two women stepped out from behind the throne.

"Korla!" Kalan exclaimed.

Gwen looked at the woman who rushed forward and embraced Kalan. Although they were twins, Gwen had come to know they were more different than alike. The other woman stayed at Conal's side. There was something odd about her, but Gwen dismissed the thought and looked at Conal. He seemed different somehow, but she wasn't sure what it was.

"You killed him," Gwen said, a statement more than a question.

"Yes," Conal replied.

Gwen nodded, remaining silent for a moment. "Was it difficult?"

"A little," he admitted. "These bone runes gave me an advantage, though."

"I meant… emotionally. Knowing that he was your—our—uncle, did that change anything?"

Conal was quiet a moment. "Not really. It's not like there was any sort of bond. And then all I had to do was remind myself that he killed my family… our family."

Gwen listened to his words, but her mind kept replaying the slaughter she'd committed. Grimmar's mages were evil, she knew, but it didn't change the fact that what she'd done had been overkill. There was something wrong with her, and she knew the dark rune was responsible. She needed to find a way to get rid of it.

Conal stopped talking and looked behind her, and she turned to see Venia and several other dragons had entered the throne room. There were a few she didn't recognize. One of them stepped forward and turned its gaze on Conal.

"We summon you to fulfill your oath." The dragon's deep voice echoed off the walls. Gwen didn't understand what that meant, and she turned back to look at her brother.

"What oath? What are they talking about? Are you in trouble?"

Gwen glanced over her shoulder at the dragons. They didn't look menacing, but there was something about their demeanors that told Gwen there could potentially be an issue. The dark rune thrummed in her veins, urging her to do insidious things.

"There's something I need to tell you. This is Derryth. Princess Derryth. She's the leader of the dragons that are left. I'm not sure how much you know about Isentol, but it was originally the home of dragons, and it's the only place where they can breed. I've agreed to hand the kingdom over to them, and we will head west to take over Tir Manach."

Gwen felt a wave of anger wash over her at the fact that Conal had agreed to give the kingdom to the dragons after all their hard work and sacrifice, but she quickly calmed herself. She didn't want to lead a kingdom, and with Torian dead, that left Conal as the only option. It made sense that he would make that decision without her, but she still felt a slight sting to her pride.

"And what of our people here? Will they be forced from their homes?"

"No," Conal reassured her. "The dragons will need our help, food, and things like that. We'll also need people who will stand up for them… here."

As things were being decided, Gwen wondered what her purpose was. If Conal was going to lead, then what would she do? Perhaps she could attempt to find a way to rid herself of the dark rune? Without anyone needing her to lead them, she would be free to do as she pleased. The idea was tempting.

"I was hoping that you might consider staying here with some of your mages," Venia said.

"Staying here with you?" Gwen asked.

"Me and my kind," Venia clarified. "We will need help and protection."

"Protection? From what? You are the most powerful creatures I've ever seen. What could possibly hurt you?"

"It surprises me how quickly humans forget," Venia said. "Do you not remember how I was almost killed? As long as my kind exists, there will always be those who seek to hunt us down."

Gwen shook her head, realizing her words probably made her sound foolish. She thought back to the previous night when the dragon hunters had mortally injured Venia with a magical weapon. Venia was right—dragons could be killed like any other species. Yet, was it her responsibility to offer that protection?

"I will consider it," Gwen said hesitantly. "There's something that I need to do before I can trust myself around others."

"The dark rune," Venia said.

"How did you know?" Gwen asked. And then she felt it. The subtle probing of her mind. "Stop doing that," Gwen said.

"You need to learn to close your mind from outside presences. If you stay here and help us, there are many things we can teach you. And maybe we can find a way to help you with the dark rune."

"Yes," Derryth chimed in. "We will help each other in beneficial ways. I will consider that the first step on the journey to building trust with humans again."

"Taking Havengarde back wasn't enough to prove that?" Gwen asked, snorting. "And where were you at? Once we entered the city, I didn't see you helping clear the way to the castle. I didn't see you fighting. You were flying safely high overhead. Many of my people lost their lives to bring Torian down. And it turns out they bled for *you,* so I think that's worth more than a few steps."

"Calm down," Kalan said gently. "She could have phrased that better, but imagine having everyone you know hunted down and killed."

"I know exactly what that's like," Gwen snapped.

"Perhaps we should talk about this elsewhere," Conal said to Derryth.

Gwen didn't care what they did. She stormed out of the throne room, fuming as she passed through the halls. By the time she exited the castle and breathed in some fresh air, she was barely holding back her tears. What was happening to her? She slumped onto the stairs and laid her head on her knees.

"It's the dark rune," Venia said from beside her. "It's infecting you from the inside."

"How do I stop it?" Gwen asked, lifting her head. The dragon had taken her elven form.

"I don't know. At least, not yet. But if we work together, I'm sure we will find a way. Dark magic is volatile, and those who use it have short lives. You've done well to control it so far, but you will need more self-control, especially if there isn't a way to rid yourself of it."

Gwen didn't want to consider that she might be forced to live with the rune for the rest of her life, but that was a possibility. She also had a decision to make. Should she live among dragons, or with her own kind? And then there was Conal. She'd lost so much time with her brother, but he was also a stranger to her. Should she go to Tir Manach with him? Could she?

"Your thoughts and emotions are at war with one another," Venia said.

"They always seem to be," Gwen muttered.

"Stay here with us," Venia said. "Take some time to rest and learn who you are."

"Rest? What is that?" Gwen laughed. "I don't think I would even know how to rest at this point." She heaved a sigh and looked out at the courtyard. "But it would be nice to do so. To have the choice."

"You do have the choice," Venia replied. "And the decision is up to you."

For the first time in a long while, Gwen felt as if that were true, as if she weren't being forced into some destiny that she had no control over. It felt … freeing. She stood up and looked at Venia.

"I'll do it," she said. "I'll stay."

CHAPTER 20

Conal

In the mid-morning daylight, Conal stood on the crest of the road where the forest ended and empty farm fields surrounding the city of Blasingdon began. The armies of Storri and Lorkan spread behind him. Above him, vultures circled the skies, waiting opportunity to descend to continue their feast on the dead.

It felt odd to be here. Well... maybe 'odd' wasn't the right word. Gwen, his sister – he'd have to get used to saying that – had remained in Havengarde, at home with the dragons and mages. Was he disappointed? Part of him had expected her to be here with him, conquering Tir Manach, then ruling as king and queen. Another part said she had her own destiny to follow.

The parting had been more than amiable, though still awkward... sort of like being forced to give a hug to an aunt you've never seen before. Yet there was a connection, a bond that they both knew and felt... and a desire to know each other better, to form the real bond of a brother and sister.

Gwen had wanted him to stick around a little longer, but he knew if he didn't strike now, opportunity would slip through his fingers. Besides, once he had conquered Tir Manach, he could come back to Havengarde anytime he wanted. There'd be time to discover who his sister really was. For now, he had another kingdom to claim.

Storri came up to stand beside him. "Doesn't look like anyone's come back."

"Would you?"

"Probably not."

They stood in silence a moment, watching the macabre display. Conal glanced at the scouts in the distance as they emerged from the forest.

"I appreciate Rorkyn lending me your help."

"I do too," the dwarf grinned. "Haven't had this much fun in a long time."

Lorkan strode up to join them. "It seems strange to come back here," he said, "at the head of an army set to conquer my own kingdom."

"*Your* kingdom?" Storri teased.

"You know what I mean."

"Change is upon us," Conal mused with a thoughtful nod. "The dragons have returned. Time for new beginnings." He twisted his head to gaze Lorkan. "You still OK with this?"

"Why shouldn't he be?" Storri interjected. "He's going to be the kingdom's army commander."

Lorkan shot him a look of irritation. "That's not why I'm doing it."

Storri shook his head and chuckled. "You two need to lighten up. Torian's evil didn't die with him. There is still work to be done. My only disappointment is that Galadyr isn't here."

"And Voldar and Torgreth," Conal added.

"Rorkyn's support only goes so far," Storri observed with a wry grin. "Besides, those two are carvers not fighters."

"Still," Conal said, stepping forward, "I'm more than thankful that you two are here. Let's see what the scouts have to tell us."

The lead scout, a short wiry man, came bustling up, dropping to his knee before Conal.

"Don't do that," Conal frowned, reaching down to touch him on the shoulder. "Just give me your report."

"Besides," Storri pointed out, "we're at war and kneeling before the king let's the enemy spies know who he is."

The man's eyes bolted wide at the obvious mistake and he gushed, "I'm so sorry, m'Lord."

"I know," Conal replied with a kind smile. "But from now on, let's just all stand and pretend like we're friends. What do you have?"

The man composed himself. "There's nothing at least two to three miles around. Seems too quiet, m'Lord. I don't like it."

"Why?"

"There should be some sort of activity, even if it was just scavengers in the city."

Conal nodded in agreement. "I know. Go ahead and push on out to Pencord."

"Yes, m'Lord." He started to bow then caught himself, unsure what to do.

"Just go," Lorkan said.

"Yes, Commander."

As the man ran off, Conal turned to a runner nearby. "Find Madlyn and bring her here."

"Yes, my Lord."

"We can't sit here all day," Storri groused.

"I know," Conal mused. "Just a couple more minutes."

He thought about his aged mage and the young Korla who decided to remain in Havengarde to gain more knowledge and power. Was he disappointed she chose to stay? Truthfully, not really. Yes, she was exceedingly attractive, but she was too… what was the word? High maintenance. Campaigning and battle were not her strong points.

Yet he was destined to be a king and a king needed a queen. Would Korla be a suitable candidate? Or should he look to align himself with another kingdom by marrying a princess? He slid a glance at Storri. *Uh… maybe I should north to the elven kingdom or east to what remains of Isentol.*

When Madlyn arrived, Conal directed her attention to the empty city.

"Not surprised," she answered. "Place is cursed. Don't see anyone living there unless they can chase away the ghosts."

"What ghosts?" Storri asked, eyes wide.

"Not them kind, dearie," she said with a smile then tapped her chest. "The ones in here. Them that lost the ones they loved won't come back." She again looed at the city. "It'll be some time before this is a city again."

Conal's attention diverted to a scout on horseback racing towards them.

"A large group on horseback approaches, my Lord," he called out as he came up.

"How large?" Lorkan interrupted.

"Couldn't tell exactly, Commander, but probably no more than a hundred."

At that moment, the newcomers emerged on the main road to Pencord. Conal grinned as they came closer.

"Seren."

"Morning, Boss," she grinned, reining in her steed and dismounting.

"Good morning, Seren. Good to see you."

She took a measure of his greeting. "You're not mad at us for not going along with you to Havengarde?"

"No." He smiled kindly at her. "Your skills are not in combat. Besides, I have other things in mind for you. Which way did you come from?"

"Came from Rexfyrd through Pencord. Thought you might could use a little intel."

"Now we're talking," Storri nodded. "What's happening?"

Seren looked quizzically at him then back to Conal.

"It's OK," Conal chuckled, shooting a bemused glance at Storri, oblivious to the breach of etiquette.

"You've a clear road through Pencord. Word's already spread that a new king arrives. A lot of folks are unhappy with Caldyr's rule and ready to join you."

"What about Rexfyrd?"

"Caldyr still controls Rexfyrd. Folks are afraid to speak out against him. He has at least a thousand soldiers in the city, with more coming from Malvyn and Pharyl."

"Pharyl?" Conal curled a lip.

"Yes, Boss." She smiled a knowing grin. "He's sent a cohort under the command of Captain Cadfyn."

"Cadfyn?" Conal smirked.

"Yeah. All told, I'd figure Caldyr's total between two thousand and twenty-five hundred."

"We still outnumber him more than two to one," Storri calculated.

"And with more joining us," Lorkan added, "we will vastly outnumber him."

"Let's move out then," Conal ordered then looked at Seren. "Ride next to me."

As the armies moved forward, Seren's small force moved in behind Conal and their leader.

"You know you can't continue as highwaymen anymore," Conal said, though scanning the positioning of his soldiers.

"We sort of figured that," she smiled. "You said you had other things in mind, Boss?"

"Yes." He turned to gazed directly at her. "I want you to be the eyes and ears within my kingdom."

"Like spies?"

"Exactly," he nodded, "with you as my spy chief."

Seren grinned, pleased. "Sounds like fun, Boss. You know you can depend on me."

"I know," he said, returning the smile. "Maldwic spoke highly of you and from what I've seen, I can trust you and you know what you're doing. Oh… one more thing."

"Yes, Boss?"

"Only you and your group may call me 'Boss.' Thus, I will know any messenger who calls me that is from you."

Seren's grin spread wider. "Thank you, Boss. This'll be fun."

Conal laughed. "I hope so."

Just as Seren had reported, the road through Pencord was uneventful except for the addition of growing numbers of citizens who wanted to join Conal's army. Conal rejected most of them on the basis that they had livelihoods to pursue and he didn't know how long the campaign would last. Besides, he didn't want to be responsible for feeding them. Still, by the time they encamped outside the walls of Rexfyrd, Conal's army had added five hundred more battle-worthy men and women.

To no one's surprise, the gates to the city were firmly shut.

Two days later, one gate door yawned open and two men and a woman slipped out. Carrying a white flag on a guidon pole, they guided their mounts to the middle of the gap separating Conal's army and the city. Alerted at the request for parley, Conal, Storri, and Lorkan rode out to meet them.

"King Caldyr demands you disband your army and leave this place," the man in the center coldly stated. He was a shorter than the other two, with close cropped hair and beard, and the manner of one used to being obeyed.

"And who are you ?" Storri offhandedly asked.

The man sat up straight in the saddle and sneered at the dwarf. "I am General Fynbear, the commander of His Majesty's army."

Storri cast an amused glance at Lorkan and stage-whispered, "Not anymore."

Bristling, Fynbear glared at them. "King Caldyr demands to know by what right you invade his kingdom. This is a peaceful realm wishing only to be left alone."

"He should have thought about that when he threw in his lot with Torian," Lorkan replied.

Fynbear narrowed his gaze at Lorkan. "I know you. You were once a loyal and true man."

"I still am," Lorkan retorted, "though not to that traitor Caldyr. I suggest you think hard about your next move. Caldyr is finished. This kingdom has a new king."

"Him?" Fynbear scoffed, ticking his head at Conal. "He is to be your king?"

"Yes," Lorkan calmly answered. "Just as he defeated Torian, he will defeat Caldyr."

"Then you – " Fynbear abruptly stopped as giant shadows flitted across the ground at the same time that cries of fear bellowed from the walls. Looking up, he cowered as two dragons circled above them then swooped down to land next to them, frightening the horses.

"Good day, m'Lord Conal," said a dragon the color of dazzling amethyst and eyes that blazed bright orange.

"Always a pleasure to see you Gawyn," Conal replied, "and you too Elys."

Elys was a dragon of equal size to Gawyn with a shimmering hue of topaz and eyes of glowing amber.

"Greetings, my Lord," Elys said, dipping his massive head.

"You two arrived just in time. I was about to explain to these individuals that it would be in their best interest to surrender the city and prevent needless death."

Gawyn turned a scaled head to the emissaries. "Tell your master that he has until the sun sets to surrender the city or we will burn it down."

Fynbear wheeled around and raced back to the gates, the other two in hot pursuit.

"How'd you know?" Conal asked as they watched the three riders slip back through the gates.

"Just a hunch," Elys said. "Thought you could use a little muscle."

"Think I'll take a little flight to remind them," Gawyn said then launched into the sky to circle ominously over the city, occasionally buzzing the guard towers.

"He's such a kid," Elys chuckled. "Think I'll join him."

Less than half-an-hour later, the dragon's threat had spread throughout the city. Not long after the news of impending conflagration had coursed it way, the gates opened wide and a prison wagon emerged, driven by a single wagoner. Crowds on foot followed behind. They stopped a short distance away. The wagoner descended and approached. As he approached, Conal knew immediately he was no ordinary merchant for he carried himself with a confident regal bearing.

"I am Prince Brody. Behind me in the wagon sits Caldyr. Do with him as you deem fit. Though I am related to him, I am not like him."

"I have heard of you," Conal said, remembering the attempts on Pharyl's life. "You have no love for your brother-in-law Pharyl."

Brody curled a lip. "He was Calder's man, Torian's man. Fortunately, I finally gained a measure of success. The city is yours to command." He bowed and stepped to the side.

"If you are not like him," Conal challenged, "why are you here?"

"I came in one last effort to make him change his mind. Instead, I was tossed in prison. Only your arrival and threat to destroy the city make my freedom possible."

Conal pondered the response. It would be easy enough to verify. "And your son, Blayne? Is he here with you?"

Brody's lips pursed. "He is dead, my Lord, a casualty of Pharyl's treachery."

"I am sorry," Conal commiserated. Dismounting, he walked up to the wagon and stared at the man inside the cage whose look of fury told him he was unrepentant.

"Confine him to the dungeon," he commanded.

"As you wish, Your Majesty," Brody said, again bowing. He flicked a hand at a man close by who leaped aboard and wheeled the wagon around. "Let me introduce you to some of the leadership of the city."

He escorted Conal along with Storri and Lorkan to a group of men and women who had positioned themselves in a line. They stopped at the first person, a middle-aged woman with darting eyes and permanent smile

"This is Lady Ailis, the burgomaster of Rexfyrd."

"Your Majesty." Ailis curtsied.

"Lady Ailis," Conal replied with a forced smile then glanced down the row, already wondering if ruling a kingdom was what he really wanted to do. He noticed a man five people down in line whose look of disapproval seemed to land on Storri. Skipping those in between, he marched down to stand in front of him.

The man was dressed as a wealthy merchant with expensive ermine and silk fitted on a portly frame. His black hair was perfectly cut and greased back.

"I couldn't help but notice your look of concern," Conal said with a smile.

The man bent forward. "It's the dwarves, Your Majesty," he said in a hushed voice. "Nothing good ever comes from dwarves."

Conal's smile vanished and his hand shot out, gripping the man by the throat and effortlessly lifting him off the ground, much to the stunned shock of the other city representatives.

"You don't like dwarves?" he growled. "The feeling is mutual. They don't like idiots."

Still holding the man aloft, he glared at the rest of them while the man's face turned redder. "Effective immediately, dwarves are to be given privileged status. If I hear of anyone disrespecting or mistreating any dwarf in my kingdom, there will be hell to pay. Understand?"

Everyone quickly nodded.

Conal felt a gentle hand on his arm.

"You may want to let him go, Dearie. Don't want to scare the neighbors."

Smiling despite himself, he lowered the man to the ground. As the man gasped for air, Conal addressed the group.

"This is Madlyn. She is the kingdom's mage. You will obey her just as you would me. To my left is Lorkan, now General Lorkan, the commander of my army. The other fine individual is General Storri, my friend and brother. Any questions?" When none came, he curtly nodded then addressed Brody. "You may escort me to my residence. And while you're doing that, I want everyone of Torian's followers rounded up. I'll deal with them on a case-by-case basis."

"Yes, Your Majesty." He motioned for Conal to follow.

"C'mon you three," Conal said to Storri, Lorkan, and Madlyn. "Let's see how the other half lives."

Conal settled on the throne and wondered if he was going to like being a king… or was it going to be all headache. People were going to go out of their way to please him, their fawning motivation being something in return. He would have to tread carefully… no changes in the beginning until he understood what was going on and how things worked.

Gazing around the throne room, he smiled at Storri and Lorkan chatting away like close friends do. Madlyn had disappeared to inspect her new home as well as call a council of mages to purge them of any residual Torian allies. The rest of the room was filled with the city's leadership, chatting amiably, all the while casting not so surreptitious glances at Conal.

Peering over the crowd, he recognized two men who stood off to the side. With a grin, he motioned them to come.

Gawyn and Elys weaved their way through the crowd and stopped at the bottom step. Conal stood and raised his hands, immediately silencing the crowd.

"You all know that the myth that dragons do not exist is not true. You have seen that for yourselves. Henceforth, anyone harming or seeking to harm a dragon will be punished by death."

The crowd audibly sucked in a breath.

"Make no mistake," Conal warned. "Dragon hunters are hereby banished from this kingdom upon pain of death. Any dragon hunter found within the borders of this kingdom by the time the morrow's sun sets has forfeited his or her life. No exceptions."

He sat back down and the thick silence gave way to quiet chatter which grew as the people relaxed.

"Tell Derryth this is a start. And thank her for letting you two help. You know you always have a place here."

"Thank you, my Lord," Gawyn said and bowed.

"Blessings on this kingdom," Elys said, "and may all your rulings be equally as wise."

With another bow, the two excused themselves to find a spot to shape change and head home to Havengarde.

Brody approached and said, "Caldyr's confidants are in the goal. Do you wish to question them now or at another time?"

"Now sounds good," Conal said, standing.

Brody led the way through the crowd, down hallways and stairways, Bedo by Conal's side.

"I was wondering where you were," Conal teased.

"I...I'm sorry, my Lord," Bedo stammered. "They wouldn't let me through. Said you already had servants. Thank the gods General Lorkan saw me."

"I do already have servants," Conal said, "which is why I need you here. You are now in charge of them all."

Bedo stumbled a step. "My Lord?"

"You are in charge of my servants. Do you not want the job?"

"Of course I do," he blurted, eyes brimming with a mixture of excitement and thanks.

"Good. We'll get things settled once I finish here."

"Yes, m'Lord."

Brody stopped at the gaoler's door and knocked. A burly bald-headed man opened it.

"His Majesty wishes to assign the prisoners," Brody announced.

"Yes, Your Majesty," the man answered with a reverent bow.

"Are we still branding people these days?" Conal questioned.

"Yes, Your Majesty."

Conal slowly nodded, hating the arbitrary exile of people to a life they did not choose nor want, yet balancing that the fact that some people needed such punishment. Hoping to find some who were repentant, he said, "Fine. As we proceed, I will tell you what brand to use or if they are to be set free. Can you write?"

The gaoler hung his head and mumbled, "No, m'Lord."

"That's fine. Lord Brody will assist us, but I bet you've a good memory."

The man brightened. "The best, Your Majesty."

"Good. Let's get started."

Conal followed the gaoler down the stone corridor to the main containment cell where more than twenty of Caldyr's loyal followers were chained to the walls.

Conal paused to gaze in through the peep hole. "Who's in here?"

"Caldyr's chamberlain, the army commander –"

"I met him already," Conal smiled. "What's your recommendation? Are there any in here who you would consider trustworthy?"

Brody thought a moment. "Honestly, Your Majesty… no."

"Good enough for me. Let's get started. Oh, by the way, we have a new category of brand."

"Your Majesty?"

"My guess is that there are few here who are worthy of the normal brands like vipers or… a rose."

Brody snorted a laugh. "Hardly, Your Majesty."

"From now on, we will now have a worker brand, a mark in the shape of a sheaf of wheat."

"As you wish, Your Majesty."

Conal was about to tell Brody to ease up on the 'Your Majesty" crap but decided to wait until he could learn more about the man.

The gaoler opened the door and commanded, "Listen up. His Majesty is entering."

Conal entered and the first man he encountered was the chamberlain, a pudgy toad of a man who bounced up.

"You Majesty," he fawned with a bow before receiving a cuff on the head from the gaoler.

"Shut yer yap. If His Majesty wants you to speak, he'll ask for it."

Conal briefly studied the man before saying "Wheat."

The chamberlain frowned, puzzled.

"Sit down," the gaoler growled.

Conal continued down the line, announcing "Wheat" with each individual, until he came to a well-dressed middle-aged man who stared back up at him with the eyes of recognition and hope.

"You," Conal pointed. "What's your name?"

"What?" the man sputtered in anger. "You know my name, damn you."

Whereupon the gaoler landed a heavy kick to the man's ribs. "That's the king yer talkin' to."

"He's not more a king than I am," the man sneered, clutching his side. "I should know."

"Then you should know to respect your betters," Brody interjected. "What is your wish, Your Majesty?"

Conal folded his arms, pretending to study the man. "Rose. Then immediately sell him to the farmers to work the fields and tend the cows and goats."

Spinning around, Conal headed to the door, the gaoler and Brody in step.

"What was his name?" Conal asked the gaoler.

"That one calls himself Lord Pharyl, Your Majesty."

Conal smirked and nodded. Being a king did have its benefits.

THE END

Thank you for joining us on this journey.
If you enjoyed it, we'd love it if you left a review!

ABOUT THE AUTHORS

Richard Fierce

Hey there!

I write fantasy and space opera, and you can find all my books in many different eBook stores. You can check out my website for more information about my books, my next projects, and events I'll be attending where you can meet me and even get signed books.

Sign up here to find out when Richard releases new books!

WEBSITE

www.richardfierce.com

FANTASY

Dragon Riders of Osnen

Trial by Sorcery

A Bond of Flame

The Warrior's Call

The Coin of Souls

Wings of Terror

Eyes of Stone

The Fallen King Chronicles
Dragonsphere
The Fallen King
The Valiant King
The Restored King

Magic and Monsters
The Wizard and the Frog

Spellbreather Novels
Smoke and Blood

Anthologies
Chronicles of Mirstone

Standalone
Shard of the Sun

SPACE OPERA
Galactic Mercenaries
Steel for Hire
Steel for Free
Steel for All

pdmac

pdmac spent a career in the US Army before transitioning to education as a university Academic Dean. He transitioned again and now writes fulltime. He has a MA in Creative Writing and a Ph.D. in Theology. He is a member of the Blue Ridge Writers Guild, the Steampunk Writers and Artists Guild, and the Georgia Writers Association. A diverse author, writer, and editor, he has also edited a Literature anthology, served as managing editor of an archaeology magazine, ghost-written an autobiography, and has had poems, short stories, articles, and editorials published in various literary journals, magazines and newspapers. His most recent short stories appear in the *Short Story America* anthologies III and IV, *Poets in Hell*, *The Mulberry Fork Review*, and the Fantasy Anthology *Chronicles of Mirstone*. He has also sung back-up for Broadway plays, provided voice for radio plays, and acted and directed theater stage productions. In his off time, he and his wife race mountain bikes, kayak, and occasionally backpack sections of the Appalachian Trail. Additionally, he and his wife love to travel, their favorite place so far being Crete, Greece.

WEBSITE
www.pdmac-author.com

FACEBOOK
www.facebook.com/pdmacauthor/

Bridge Quest: A GameLit Adventure Series

Bridge Quest

Orc's Bane

Lord of Innis Torr

The Sci Fi/Fantasy Series Wolf 359:

Wolf 359

Queen to Play

A Once and Future King

The Puppet King

The Templar Rebellion

Wolf 359 – Box Set

Steampunk Western: Tombstone Series

Fool's Gold

An Ounce of Lead

The Devil's Disciple (Spring 2021)

Viking Time Travel Romance

Beyond Her Touch

A Dystopian Novel:

Rebirth of Angels

A Time Travel Novella
Ctrl Z: The Do Over Stone

Poetry
a young man no more